WHERE WOLVES PROWL

A gripping Scottish mystery

JAMES ANDREW

Published by The Book Folks

London, 2022

ISBN 978-1-80462-008-3

www.thebookfolks.com

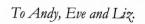
To Andy, Eve and Liz.

PROLOGUE

A blur of naked limbs tumbling. A splash. A thrash of legs pushing at water.

A pool. Evening. Light glancing through air, through water. Pale concrete slabs support black loungers, one of which has been overturned. Dark streams of blood spill out into the water. A body jerks with its memories of being alive, before finally growing still. The sound of the churn of water stops. A crow caws as if mocking something. The body is face down in the water, blood still seeking out a new home. Its limbs point outwards and down. Everything about the body points away from air, from light.

The sound of a laugh scrawls itself across air. It reaches a hysterical pitch then quietens itself.

A voice calls out. 'So, that was all it took?'

The laugh returns, as if rearing in triumph, then cuts itself off abruptly.

Music is thrumming out from somewhere in the background but only now becomes noticeable as voices in that elsewhere mingle. Their laughter surges with a lightness that has nothing to do with a body thrashing in water.

Close by, there is the sound of footsteps as if someone has just left the scene.

ONE

So, here Jason was, in Nairn, waiting to see what might happen next. Nairn was a seaside town, and he could hope that living in an outward-looking place would give him a feeling of optimism again. He liked the view of waves and sky when he walked along the front, and he enjoyed the tang of the sea and the coolness of the breeze. There was a beach and there were outdoor cafés. Tourists strolled about, and the sound of children laughing echoed round. Nairn held all the charms of a holiday resort.

It might have been his imagination but Nairn seemed to have far more sunny days than Edinburgh. He seemed to be always taking advantage of the weather to wander round the seafront, and this was an unusually warm May day.

An outdoor café stood beside a putting green near some tall trees. People sat round its tables, drinking coffee, eating cake, or licking ice cream, and there were always queues at the counter.

When he could, he strolled to it in the morning; he would bring a newspaper and sip an Americano as he read it. Because he hadn't been in Nairn that long – only a few months – he tended to be left to himself, which allowed him to observe other people when he wasn't reading about bombings and other goings-on in the world. One group of people was absorbing his attention.

They were the kind who dripped money; it oozed from the lightness of their laughter, the careless way they draped themselves on their chairs, and the cattiness of remarks that drifted across. Even the clothes they wore suggested affluence, not that they were obviously expensive – it was casual clothing they wore – but closer inspection showed the brand names peeking from the corners were designer, and the watches and jewellery they wore were a flash of wealth.

It was the women who first drew Jason's attention. He was sure he had never come across a whole set of young ladies quite as attractive as they were. A glow came from them, as if their soft skins had been tended in hothouses. These bodies had not lacked nutrition, had not been nurtured by chips and fried chicken, or microwaved dinners. No trans-fats lay unhealthily beneath those skins, bloating arms and torsos. When they walked about, they moved like dancers; there was grace in everything they did.

They knew how attractive they were. The glances they shot around were the looks of models aware of the effect they produced, as might be seen on the cover of *Vogue* or *Elle*, not that Jason recognized any of them from a cover, but that was their physical type: elegant, willowy, with angular cheeks, and startling eyes, though not one glance was given in Jason's direction. It was as if he wasn't there, which suited him. It was peace and quiet he wanted, and he embarrassed himself enough by noticing them.

But he couldn't stop himself glancing in their direction. Laughter peeled out from them like music; it drifted out in waves, soaring and dipping as if orchestrated, and their faces were lit as if by lamps from within.

He thought that, if he'd been an artist, he would have preserved them for ever on those seats under the trees in the summer sunshine, light dappling through the leaves. They were a moment of lightness to be held onto. He knew however that, in reality, such moments don't last, and they are often mirages.

He wondered if that was what these people were, false impressions created by his over-imaginative mind. They seemed so carefree, an image of happiness, but perhaps

3

they were not so beautiful, or relaxed; underneath these studied attitudes could lurk unresolved tensions ready to explode into violence at any moment.

The men with them were not the type that Jason wished to know; their laughter brayed out an arrogance Jason had always found difficult. It was as if money had given them an offhand relationship with a world that was expected to know its place and accept their assumption of superiority, though Jason didn't know anyone who kowtowed to that sort of thing, and he certainly didn't.

They were tall, healthy young people – of about his own age, but who moved and behaved in such a more relaxed way – and their laughter continued to spill out.

Two of them separated themselves from the others, a man and woman who strolled over to a Tesla car parked in front of the Royal Marine Apartments. The car was white, shiny, and sleek, designed for speed.

They opened the doors and eased themselves in, vigorous, careless, and looking forward to the opportunities in life their backgrounds had prepared them for. Jason couldn't help hoping there was something wrong with this picture; he wanted life to hold revenge somewhere round the corner for all that apparent privilege.

One person in the set stood out; he discovered later her name was Isla Robertson Landy. For all that the whole group exuded physical good looks, when Jason looked at Isla's face, he could see that there was something awkward in the way it was put together. Perhaps the eyes or the mouth were too large, but only in a way that compelled attention, and made her seem even more attractive than if the features had been more regular. The eyes had a hypnotic effect, that Isla put to good use when she decided to dominate a conversation. And her legs! When she stretched them out in her seat, they seemed to go on forever. This was a slim young lady in the prime of her beauty, and, as far as Jason could see, she knew it.

When her laugh stretched itself out as well, it was with a joyful flourish that was deliberate. Isla was a woman aware of every gesture and sound she made. And Jason was fascinated by her.

Then she walked over and introduced herself to him.

* * *

Jason Sutherland had always hated his name. It didn't fit together. Jason didn't feel like a Scottish name; it belonged to a classical Greek figure in a plumed helmet, wielding a sword, and the name Sutherland belonged to a drover in a tartan plaid. Though that summed him up in a sense; there was something about him that didn't fit together in the way it might be expected to.

The fact he lived in Nairn was odd. He wasn't quite sure what he was doing there. He wasn't brought up in Nairn and had no family anywhere near. He had been born in Edinburgh, gone to school and university there, and had started off his teaching career in one of the local city schools.

The school he had attended as a pupil had been one of the local comprehensives, which had always felt a disadvantage as so many youngsters in Edinburgh go to independent schools like Loretto or The Royal High – not that Jason thought there was anything wrong with his local comprehensive. There couldn't have been. He went to it. But disadvantage seemed to sum up Jason's life. He was brought up in an apartment block by his mother on her own. She taught him to speak properly, to have ambitions, and to behave better than the other children nearby because she said he had well-to-do relatives, though Jason hadn't seen any of them, except one cousin of his mother's, who visited from time to time, wearing expensive clothes and scent and an air of charity. She was kind at least, and Jason noticed that they were better off for a while after her visits. When he'd finished his probationary period and was a fully qualified teacher, he had a hankering to see what life was like on the other side of the fence; with the self-opinion his mother had given him he'd never fitted in where he was.

It was partly how he had had ended up teaching at Rose High School, an independent school near Nairn, which was a completely different experience to the school where he'd taught in Edinburgh. Its pupils were less intense and not in the least disadvantaged, and it was good to be receiving a less torrid time as a teacher. There was the thought it might even help him advance his career.

The other reason was one he had great difficulty in discussing.

He hadn't brought much with him: two suitcases' worth of belongings, and as few memories as he could manage. No encumbrances.

He wasn't a complete loner by instinct; even now he did make a sort of attempt to keep up with former friends, but there was a part of himself that had to be kept away from others.

He was a good teacher. He knew that, even though he was still developing, as he'd only been teaching for a couple of years. It wasn't something he'd learned at teacher training college or from other teachers that had helped him. It was something his mother had said.

She had quoted a poem to Jason. Jason hadn't realised his mother was interested in poetry, but she knew this poem, *If*— by Rudyard Kipling, which was old-fashioned even for his mother but meaningful to him. 'If you can keep your head when all about you are losing theirs and blaming it on you, if you can trust yourself when all men doubt you, but make allowance for their doubting too… you'll be a Man, my son!'

Oddly enough, it worked, when he made use of it in his teaching of classes, or when he attempted to. He overheard one of his pupils commenting on him once. The boy had said, 'If you just don't react to them, that gives you power over your classes. Or that's what he does.'

Which was Jason's Rudyard Kipling impersonation. Jason had a professional lack of emotion in crisis situations, and a steady, authoritative voice, and his pupils fell for it.

He sometimes wondered if he found it too easy to do; he did worry about himself at times. Fellow teachers with a similar amount of experience allowed themselves to become so upset by difficult pupils. Perhaps, Jason thought, he was cold-blooded, though he was sure he hadn't always been like that. How had that happened?

But he knew the answer to that. It was the man he'd killed that had done that to him, the justifiable murder he'd got away with. That was what cut him off from other people now.

Jason had been engaged to be married at one time, and there had been close friends, but he was unable to do closeness with anyone now. He'd told himself he'd travelled to Nairn for a job but that wasn't true. He'd come there to leave things behind, the thing he did and anyone who might know anything about that, but it had been impossible to leave his memories behind.

He supposed it was why he felt half-dead inside. He was a man trapped inside frozen emotions. He wondered if anyone did come to terms with killing another human being.

He'd left so much in the attempt to leave that behind and find escape and healing in Nairn, and he wasn't prepared for Isla.

* * *

As far as Jason was aware, no one in that set had so much as glanced in his direction, and he often sat near them, so it was a shock when Isla walked over to him and spoke. She gave him the clearest view of expensive-looking and dazzlingly white teeth as she aimed her slightly lopsided smile at him and he became aware of the effect of a full blast from Isla's eyes, and the fact they were a startling shade of violet.

'Why do you stare so much?' she said.

'I don't,' Jason replied. 'Or at least I'm sure I don't.'

'You've been gawping at us forever.'

'Really? I am sorry. I didn't mean to.'

'You definitely have been,' she said. 'Not that we mind. It's flattering that anyone should find us interesting at all. We're just us. Boring old us. So, are you strange?' she asked.

'Now there's a question,' he said. 'I've never been asked that before. Why on earth do you ask?'

'You're always on your own. And you stare.'

'I don't mean–' he said, and gathered his jacket as he readied himself to put it on and leave.

'You don't need to go. We have asked around about you,' she said, 'and the popular opinion is that you're harmless – or relatively so. So, you don't need to depart in a hurry. You can stay.'

Now the violet eyes did full work on him, wielding irresistible charm, along with the full-on smile.

'You've not lived in Nairn long, so you don't know anybody. You only arrived here in January. That's why you're always on your own. It sounds reasonable enough. And you teach at Rose High School, which suggests someone thinks you're safe.'

Jason couldn't prevent himself from giving a short laugh. There was something so impudent in this critique from a stranger. But then wasn't it the conceit of this group that had fascinated him from the beginning? And here it was right in front of him displaying itself in all its magnificence, like a peacock showing off its tail feathers. He had never met anyone who attempted to work charm on him in that way, if Isla was trying to do that, though the violet eyes appeared to be switched off now, even if the smile wasn't.

'We couldn't help noticing you hanging around. And we all suggested different things about you. Andy thought there was something desperate in you as if you're on the run. Are you?'

Jason found himself choking but did not answer.

'You are?' Isla said. 'That's interesting. We do have local police if you want them pointed in your direction.'

'I'm not on the run.'

Jason found the words rushing out of him.

'Andy's the six-footer, the one with the muscles. If he suggests you're running away from anything, I'd agree. Now, Joanne – she's the redhead – she thinks you look interesting and pale as if you've been unlucky in love. And there are a lot of dreadful women out there. We ought to know. We are.'

'I'm sure you're not,' Jason said.

'Oh, but we are,' Isla said. 'Definitely.'

She not only unleashed her perfect teeth on him now but the eyes again.

'Ellie – she's the one with the outrageous glasses – she thinks you're on the run because of your debts. She fantasises that you spend time in expensive casinos being bamboozled by roulette wheels and watered-down champagne. But I'm sure you're too intelligent for that.'

'Between all of you, you're writing quite the novel about me,' Jason replied. 'Is it likely to be published any time soon? Because I fancy reading it.'

'And then there's my husband. Yes. I've got one of those, and he is sometimes around. That's Paul. The other six-footer. The one with the barrel chest. He thinks you're probably just one of the mass unemployed. Or he did. Until we asked around about you. I said it might be more interesting if you were. Teaching in a school is so boring, isn't it?'

'I wouldn't say that.'

'Not that you've been around long enough to find out if that one is or isn't.'

'It seems a nice school.'

9

'How very… nice,' Isla said. She paused. 'And you really don't know a soul, do you?'

But she didn't give Jason the chance to reply to that.

'How sad. But we can't allow you to be a sad person, with nothing to do but watch groups of silly folk like us. We must help you get to know some people at least. Tell you what. There's a party on at my house tonight. Why don't you come round? About seven?'

Jason was taken aback. She was, despite his misgivings, being friendly. And a party sounded fun.

'OK,' he said.

'OK? Is that it? OK?'

'And thanks. And perhaps you should tell me where your house is?'

'Don't you know? Perhaps you don't. Everyone else around here does. It's on the front. The terribly modern-looking eco-house with the big flashy windows looking out to sea.'

'That one?' Jason said.

He did recognize it. Who wouldn't? And that was where Isla lived?

'It's just a pool party,' she said. 'But they're fun, don't you think?'

Jason supposed so though he had never been to one.

'You could get to know us better,' Isla said. 'You seem to find us fascinating enough. Or if you do find us boring when you get to know us, you could always meet other people. There will be others there. Or might be.'

'Thanks again for the invite,' he said.

'It's a pleasure,' she said and the assault of the violet eyes suggested she might even mean it.

'I look forward to coming along.'

'We look forward to seeing you,' Isla said. 'My name's Isla by the way.'

Which is when he finally found out what she was called.

'Isla Robertson Landy.'

It rang a bell. How could it not? This fascinating creature was Isla Robertson Landy? Not that Robertson was in any way a noticeable name, but Landy was. Robertson must be her husband's name. It was interesting that she should also have kept her father's. Landy was a famous name in Nairn and everywhere else probably. Her father must be Mark Landy, the Scottish film star. Everyone in Nairn knew about him. That was his house on the shore? Though Jason had known Mark Landy had lived in Nairn he had never known where. He thought he was probably the only one who didn't. He supposed it figured it would be that one. It was expensive and striking enough.

Then Isla floated off, back to her friends, with no backward glances. They continued to contrive to look bored as if they hadn't even noticed she had come over to talk to him, never mind that she'd just returned.

Jason didn't know what to think about Isla; she put on a good act, he just wasn't sure what it was.

* * *

Jason started strolling back to his modest, ill-lit, and cramped two-bedroom flat in Nairn. He usually walked along the central beach and then up towards the centre of town. This time he headed in a different direction. He walked west along the promenade and past the posh houses set on their headland looking steadfastly out to sea. Some were bungalows if not particularly modest ones. Others were grand Victorian properties with Gothic towers, standing amongst trees, and looking as if all they needed to complete the picture they presented as doubles for vampire castles were the vampires themselves and swarms of bats. Lightning and thunder would have helped the picture too. Some were of more recent constructions; one standing out, angular and modern, with huge picture windows, and Jason thought that must be the one described by Isla Robertson Landy. When Jason came up to it, he stopped and stared.

Now this was a house. The garden in front of it tumbled down the slope with almost nonchalance. There were concrete steps there leading down to an iron gate, and there was grass, resplendently green, and manicured. There were shrubs with delicately coloured flowers. Jason was surprised that anyone managed to cut the lawn so neatly on that slope. The whole place looked as if it was attended by an army of servants – and probably was.

Glass gleamed from everywhere in the building; it was a lighthouse of reflection in the noonday sun. What wasn't glass was white, polished, painted concrete; the white searingly perfect. The roof was flat. The building was a beacon of modernity and fashion, as if it was designed to blazon its desirability to the world.

Two wings, rounded in a manner reminiscent of art deco, stretched toward the firth on either side of a courtyard that was made of the same white concrete. Seats lounged around on it, and pot plants wafted fronds around. Both wings had large walls facing the sea that were made of glass and the interior could be seen easily. The one on the left was a kitchen and dining area, and the one on the right a living area. Behind the central court area was a pool, placid behind the glass.

Jason thought what an oasis of calm that courtyard would be. There would be no hiding from any breeze coming straight off the sea, but easterly, westerly, and southerly winds were catered for, and Jason knew the glass wall in front of the pool would slide back, to turn it into an outdoor pool when desired. Jason had seen someone lounging by it before.

A pool party there appealed to him. He looked at his iPhone and checked the weather for the evening. The wind was set in a favourable direction, and sunshine and warmth were forecast. There was never a guarantee of this in

Scotland which was why the pool could be converted to an indoor one, but that evening beckoned kindly.

Jason told himself to stop staring. He'd been told off once for that already that day. He strolled past and continued on his way home. He turned up Seabank Road, then turned left along Thurlow Road and behind the houses he'd been admiring from the seafront. The West End of Nairn was a desirable area. Every one of the large stone houses he passed on his left could be described as a mansion.

But Jason's feet soon led him to the joys of the A96 bludgeoning its way through the middle of present-day Nairn. His walk was now punctuated by the sound of car horns; and there were idling cars impatient for the chance to move forward. He found himself looking at one of Nairn's infamous traffic queues. Irate faces glanced at him from car windows while raucous music blared from radios. Jason found himself muttering as he waited for the chance to cross the road. When it came, he seized it, then found himself outside a block of flats built for functionality rather than any pretence at style.

Jason took out his keys and let himself into a dark stairway, trudged up it, opened his front door and threw himself on the couch in the worn-looking living room. He closed his mind to the clutter he'd left lying around and tried to rediscover the peace of mind he'd found when lounging along the Nairn seafront.

TWO

As he waited for seven o'clock to come around, Jason found it difficult to settle down to anything. He spent time preparing himself, though for what he still wasn't sure.

He showered, trimmed eyebrows, nose hair, and nails. Did rich people pay attention to that sort of thing? You bet, he thought. He also slapped on his latest aftershave, which had cost a whole ten pounds, and probably smelt as much of its alcohol base as anything else, but Jason lived in hope. He shrugged on a navy-blue cotton shirt and black chinos, then fastened his black Swatch onto his wrist, wishing it was a Rolex. He finished by putting a black agate and silver ring on one of the fingers of his right hand. Casual but flashy, huh? he said to himself.

As he admired himself in the mirror, he had to admit he thought he looked OK. Though he did wonder if he looked like someone who deserved to be invited to a pool party at Mark Landy's. The word cheap applied itself somewhere – if not everywhere.

He could not even harbour physical pretensions. He was five foot nine, which is not tall. His hair was mousy and his skin sallow. His features were regular though hardly striking, and he was a bit too lean. He knew he could do with bulking up with some muscle. No. He didn't cut the required dash in swimming trunks, but he was going to have to do. He didn't have any other body to wear.

He'd been asked to arrive at seven and he gave thought to that. He didn't think it would do to be too early, or particularly late. Perhaps if he arrived at about five past he would project the right level of coolness, if he could manage any at all at this sort of party.

* * *

The entrance to the house was along Thurlow Road, a tree-lined row of majestic stone properties. Villa Pleasance was the name Mark Landy had given to his mansion, which Jason thought was after a property in one of Mark's movies. It was set at the end of a long, gated drive. There was a buzzer to the side of the gate. After Jason had pressed it, he heard the whirr of a camera turning to look at him. Then the gate opened itself and closed smartly behind him after he had entered.

Before he reached the house, he had to walk down a slope past quite a forest of Scots pines to the entrance. From this side of the house, less glass and more concrete could be seen. The door opened as he came up to it, and Isla welcomed him. She showed him into a hallway which was impressive in height, and was dominated by a spiral staircase, then led Jason through to the pool area.

Draped over reclining loungers was an impressive array of half-naked female bodies, most of which he recognized from the café on the front even without clothes as they were now.

Isla turned and looked him up and down.

'It's a pool party,' she said. 'You're overdressed.'

She pointed to a door. He went into the small bedroom behind it and changed. When he emerged in his black boxer swimming trunks, and walked over to the pool area, he put on a smile, as much carelessness as he could manage, and tried to pretend he wasn't doing this. Pairs of female eyes followed him as he flopped onto an empty lounger. Feeling he had been found duly inadequate, he flipped sunglasses on and hid behind those. At least it was warm in such a sheltered spot.

Isla gave him an easy smile.

'Welcome to the gang,' she said.

He managed a sort of grin in return.

'So, this is Ellie,' she said, flicking her hand towards probably the dumpiest female there – and she only looked slightly plump because the rest were so slim.

She wore a suggestion of a swimsuit that seemed to be designed to show as much cleavage and leg as possible. Her hair looked recently sprayed and she hadn't been in the pool. With that make-up and bottled tan she wasn't there to splash about.

'Ellie works at Gordonstoun.'

Jason was impressed by the light mention of that name.

'As a teaching assistant though. Nothing grand. Considering the mint her parents spent on her education, they must feel short-changed. They do, don't they, Ellie? You have a very posh accent though, don't you?'

Isla gave her a blasé smile.

Ellie gave one in return as she said, 'Fuck off, Isla.'

Isla was right. The cut-glass vowels were obvious.

'And this is Joanne.'

Joanne was slight, with short-cut brunette hair and a surprisingly thoughtful look for a girl on a lounger in a swimsuit. She gave Jason an inquiring simper, then turned it off.

'Joanne's the intellectual one. She passed some exams. Very clever. Of course, it was only in creative writing, not anything heavy. But she is qualified to teach the stuff at university – on paper. Though she would have to get something published first, wouldn't you, Joanne?'

'It'll happen, Isla.'

'Yes, but not anytime soon. You need to write it first before someone can publish it, Joanne.'

'You do know you're going to be a corpse in one of my novels, Isla?'

'So you keep threatening.'

Isla turned to Jason and put a confidential look on her face.

'Unemployed. Claims to be writing the great British novel,' she said to him.

She turned to another girl.

'And this is Lena.'

A blonde with a face that looked as if it was fixed in a permanent smile waved at Jason. He waved back. He was pleased to be introduced to anyone who looked like her. Lena was pale with a body that went in and out in the places it should, and her swimsuit just covered them.

'She looks as if she hasn't a brain in her head but don't believe the vacuous smile. It's taken a lot of practice to perfect that. Lena's sharp as a razor, aren't you, Lena?'

Lena smirked even more widely but said nothing.

'She teaches A level Maths – also at Gordonstoun. Not that I expect the boys learn much of that. They're more interested in a different sort of figure.'

Lena did not deign to answer this time either.

'Actually, we all went to school at Gordonstoun as kids,' Isla continued, 'which is how we know each other, though why anyone would want to teach there I can't imagine. I do teach too – Art, part-time – but certainly not there.'

She flipped her hand towards a gamine-like young woman with short, brunette hair and delicate features that looked as if they would grace a doll.

'And this is Amber. Amber's an actress, aren't you, Amber? Aspiring anyway. She's at RADA. So, you'd have to ask what on earth she's doing up here. Not that you can usually believe anything Amber says. She's always in part for something.'

Amber looked as if she understood she was there to be talked at, not to participate in the conversation.

'And that's the crew,' Isla said. 'Oh, and the men. You'll be glad to see you're not the only one. The one about to dive in – I've told you before, but I'd better remind you. That's Paul, my husband. He doesn't do very much apart from swim about. He says he's between jobs.

He's a journalist so-called, and he does do some freelance work now and again.'

'I'm pleased to meet him,' Jason said.

'And the seal swimming up and down' – Isla flopped her arm in the direction of the other swimmer – 'in case you've forgotten, is Andy. I've already warned you not to argue with him. You'd find he likes it too much. He's a legal eagle. Works for a big firm in Aberdeen. Says he's very up and coming. We're surprised they hired him. So there we are' – she gave a smug smile as she turned to Jason – 'the crew.'

Then she turned away from Jason and gestured to them.

'Oh, and this is the strange man from the café – Jason. Say hello to Jason, everybody.'

'Hi Jason,' came from a variety of voices.

'Hi,' Jason said.

'And your side table is empty,' she said. 'It's missing its cocktail. On offer are a Manhattan or a Shady Lady. Though I should warn you, if you order a Shady Lady, you might get one of us instead.'

'Tempting though that sounds, I think I'll have a Manhattan,' Jason said.

'Wise choice.'

Isla floated over to a tabled area, found some bottles, and a glass, and mixed them into a cocktail shaker. She soon returned with the Manhattan. Now that it had been pointed out to him, Jason noticed the half-empty glasses beside the other loungers.

A voice floated over.

'So, what's it like teaching the hoi polloi?'

That had come from Lena, who then giggled. Jason had to stop himself grimacing. The easy suggestion of superiority that emanated from these people was beginning to grate already.

'At Rose High School?' he replied.

'But you taught in Edinburgh in a comprehensive, didn't you?'

Jason wondered how she could have known that.

'It's just teaching human beings,' he said.

'I taught in comprehensives when I did my teacher training,' Lena said, 'and I'm not sure that some of my pupils were. I don't miss them.'

'You can't lump them all together in your mind,' Jason replied.

'They seemed to want to give me a particularly tough time of it.'

'Maybe you were unlucky.'

'I didn't get that impression.'

Then Lena giggled again, and Jason could not think why. Did she have a Marilyn Monroe affectation?

'So, why did you come to this neck of the woods?' another voice pealed out.

That was Amber who seemed to be practising her fascinating look as she said it.

'I was offered a job,' Jason said. 'A teacher needed replacing because of health issues.'

'But why apply for one here?' Amber said.

Jason paused as he tried to think how to reply. 'It seemed a good idea at the time,' he said, then tried not to feel too embarrassed at how weak the answer was.

'Didn't you like the job you were in before?'

'I didn't mind it, but it was time for a change.'

'And you came all the way to sunny Nairn. Where was it you said you're from again?' she asked.

Conversation continued like this for a while. People made casual queries and Jason answered them or fielded them as he wished. Despite the infuriating manner this set possessed, they were polite enough, their curiosity casual and without malice, and they chatted happily about themselves in return. The thing that linked all of them was that privileged background.

Jason started to form a stronger impression of each. Ellie was the least relaxed, as if she worked to fit in with this set. Her father, Jason learned later, was a high-earning barrister, whom Jason had heard of. He defended high-profile criminals and his last case had made him notorious. He had got a criminal off a murder charge on a technicality. Perhaps a sense of shame made Ellie anxious to please.

The most natural was the actress, Amber Lennox. Maybe she was in part as herself tonight. With her acting parents, she might be so used to celebrity parties this was the equivalent of slumming it. Jason would have liked to meet her father; he had often been in Jason's living room on his TV as a famous sleuth.

Joanne intrigued Jason because of the effortless stream of words that flowed from her, and the non-stop work she put her smile muscles through. With her prettiness, she dazzled, though it puzzled Jason that anyone should feel the need to impress quite so much, and he wondered at the occasional hesitancy when she talked to Isla.

Lena's constant, high-pitched giggle made for an irritating backdrop, though the timing suggested it was thoughtfully done.

When Paul himself strolled over, Jason was impressed by his offhand charm. There was a calmness in his manner that stood out, but when Paul turned to Isla, something changed. A stiffness appeared in him, and Isla seemed to tense; there was an undercurrent there. It was odd there should be that frisson between husband and wife. Jason might have thought they'd be more relaxed with each other.

When Andy imposed himself on the conversation there was a hint of an aggression that put people on the defensive, particularly Paul, Jason noticed.

Isla continued to project her casual charm at them all – and Jason continued to fall for it.

Overall, though, despite the affability of this set, Jason had the impression there was something he couldn't quite catch – and wasn't meant to.

As the evening progressed, the Manhattans continued to flow, and the laughter became more raucous. People continued to swim the odd length of the pool. It was just after Jason had hauled himself dripping back to his lounger that Mark Landy appeared, with, beside him, his wife and fellow actor, Lily Hagen, whom Jason recognized from other Hollywood blockbusters.

Mark was not dressed for the pool. He was wearing a white tee shirt and black chinos, a gold chain round his neck, and a Rolex on his wrist. His black hair was immaculate as was his smile, which he beamed immediately he entered the pool area. Mark was a tall man, and muscular as befitted an action film star; his skin was tanned, and he glowed health.

'Hi, Isla.' He grinned. 'You've brought friends round again.'

'You made such a point of the architect including a pool in his plans, it would be a shame not to use it.'

Though the words were bold, Isla was not displaying the same sangfroid now that she addressed her father. The glance she gave him indicated almost subservience.

'It's good to see. Everyone having a good time?'

He flashed his smile around again. In reply, murmurs of agreement rippled round.

'Keep it up,' he said.

'We intend to,' Isla said.

'You've had enough practice,' Lily said. 'Do you ever do much else?'

As it was said lightly, the remark might not have meant much, but, all the same, something in the note in Lily's voice jarred with the general tone of the conversation. Jason took it there was no love lost between her and Isla. Isla contented herself with a challenging look in answer.

'You really ought to do something about that hair of yours, Isla. That's last year's style. I've told you before.'

Isla gave her a sweet smile that could have cut its way through concrete.

'Do enjoy yourself with my father. But give him some rest now and again. He isn't getting any younger – either.'

'Isla,' Mark said. 'Behave yourself.'

Isla now gave him the same smile.

Jason's eyes flitted between the two women. In appearance they were opposites, Lily with her honey-blonde hair and pale skin, and Isla with her black hair and olive complexion. Jason felt his eyes could have lingered on them forever. By a hair's breadth, he thought, Isla was probably the more beautiful. It was the violet eyes. More beautiful than a leading film actress? Isla might be wasting her life teaching.

'You're going somewhere?' Paul asked Mark.

'I've a filming schedule,' Mark replied, 'and a plane booked for tonight. But it won't be long till I'm back. The filming's nearly finished.'

Jason wondered what the film could be. Another Danger Team movie? The franchise was massive, and Jason always watched them.

'And you look after my little girl while I'm away, Paul.'

'She's hardly that anymore,' Paul said.

'After all, you've nothing else to do.'

Now it was Mark's turn to be cutting. Jason noticed that his grin was wider when he said the words, which reminded Jason of scenes in Mark's films where he was about to finish off the villain. That was when Mark put on his widest smile. Paul seemed to take the remark in his stride, but Jason winced for him.

'Not true,' Paul said. 'I've been commissioned to do an article for a Sunday.'

'You have?'

And it was obvious Mark did not believe this.

'On developments in the Speyside whisky industry.'

Mark gave him another grin, but it was toned down a bit from his deadly one. Perhaps he gave Paul the benefit of the doubt.

'I look forward to reading it,' he said. 'Which newspaper is it?'

'The Mail on Sunday.'

'Impressive,' Mark said.

'He doesn't spend all his time lounging by the pool, really, Dad.'

Isla's smile was a simper now. Mark swept a vague, but broad grin round the rest of the company.

'I envy you all,' he said. 'A nice evening like this, and nothing to do but enjoy it. While I need to fight six bad guys at once – again.'

'And kiss pretty actresses, Dad.'

'In my films I spend a lot more time defending myself against stunt men than doing that.'

'You get to meet Gabrielle D'Astagne,' Paul said. 'I'd give my right arm to work with her.'

'You stick to my daughter and behave yourself,' Mark said.

The remark was casual but Jason couldn't help noticing the deadly grin had returned. Mark and Paul did not get on – either. It occurred to Jason that he had never been in a company where despite the display of cordiality there were such tensions.

'And don't get too plastered,' Mark said as he gave a glance round the pool. 'You'll make me jealous.'

Which was an attempt at friendliness. Mark Landy didn't drink – at least according to his publicity. Then Mark seemed to notice Jason for the first time.

'And hi,' he said.

'Hi,' Jason replied.

What do you say to a film star? Jason asked himself. Hi. Was that it? But he couldn't think of anything else.

'This one's new,' Mark said to Isla.

Lily Hagen's eyes swivelled towards Jason for the first time. Her eyes were a light hazelnut, not that Jason usually paid that much attention to the colour of someone's eyes. It must be something to do with actors and acting families. Their eyes seemed to draw him in, particularly Lily Hagen's. It was as if her whole vitality was on display in them, and Jason was struck by it. There was such a sense of piercing intelligence. Lily's eyes read deep inside him, as if wondering if he should be dismissed or accepted.

'He's a stray,' Isla said. 'We found him at a café on the front. He looked lonely so we brought him here to cheer him up.'

'Be careful how you go,' Mark said to Jason. 'Pretty young ladies aren't as harmless as they look.'

'He's a local teacher,' Isla said.

But Mark's interest in Jason had already gone. It hadn't lasted long, Jason thought.

'I have to leave,' Mark said.

He gave the room one last smile, turned, and departed, Lily in tow. She must be jetting off to the film set as well. Was she in this movie too? Jason wondered. Probably. She was in the last one Mark had done.

That was the extent of Jason's first conversation with Mark Landy, and there wasn't a lot for Jason to tell his grandchildren there. He would have to make something up. But he'd been impressed by Mark. As a celebrity he was the one with most call to put on airs and graces, but he had been the least affected there.

Then they were left to themselves and the first thing Isla did was top up everybody's Manhattans. Jason wondered what had happened to the Shady Ladies but decided that probably had been banter. This time he watched her preparing a cocktail and was surprised by the amount of spirits it took, at least the way Isla made them.

Then another two guys and a girl turned up. Everybody already knew them. With their accents and clothes, they could have been others in the set, except they carried a couple of guitars with them – and a mike and speakers. This was the band. The girl sang while the guys strummed. They played a sort of soulful blues rock. The girl's voice was melodic and strong, and she enjoyed making the most of it. What was most memorable though was what they had brought with them; there was now a good supply of cocaine to go with the cocktails. Jason noticed that hadn't turned up until Mark Landy had gone. Jason put his Manhattan down, walked over to the poolside and dived in. As he didn't do drugs, he needed to work this out.

Jason did his usual crawl the length of the pool and back, surprised at how much his cocktail had affected him. He should go before the evening became too wild, not that he wanted to. He had never known people such as these. They were so self-possessed in the way they carried themselves, but there was something relaxing about being in their company. Then there was Isla. Perhaps he could flop onto a lounger, continue to enjoy the scene, and just refuse the drugs.

The last thing he remembered of the evening was taking a long pull of his glass while gazing at Isla. He knew she was already taken – with Paul, lucky man – but Jason could enjoy the view. And she did seem to have become more beautiful somehow as the evening went on. She had noticed the way Jason was looking at her though he had tried not to make it obvious. What did the mischievousness in her smile mean? He could hope she was admiring him but knew that wouldn't happen. Then she began to drift out of focus, and Jason noticed that was happening with everything else he looked at too. Then he woke up next morning.

THREE

As Jason surfaced, he became aware of a headache and weary limbs, Isla's voice in his head, and her lovely face with its lopsided grin as she talked to him.

'Do you know the thing that's most striking about you?' she asked.

'What?'

'Your smile.'

That was something Jason was not aware of.

'It doesn't work properly,' she said.

'It doesn't?'

'Your lips sort of try to lift at the sides of your mouth as if they might be going to grin but they don't quite make it.'

'Really?'

And now Isla was unleashing hers – and there was no problem with it.

'It's sort of as if you've forgotten how to. Have you?'

He replied with his sort of half-smile and the remark, 'I'm not aware of anything wrong with my foolish grin.'

'Something's happened,' Isla said. 'Something went wrong and made you like that. And you should let me help you with it. I want to see you smiling properly again. One thing we do know in our family is how to smile. It's important. It helps other people relax. Don't you know that?'

If he hadn't, he did now. He gazed at Isla and thought she was the most wonderful creature he'd ever met in his life. But she couldn't have said any of that; that was the dream he'd woken up with the next day.

He groaned and stretched. He was at home in his rumpled bed with the curtains closed and the smell of sleep around him. He pulled himself out of bed and put on his dressing gown. He wandered over to the window and pulled the curtains open.

Sun streamed in. The sky was blue with suggestions of white clouds. It was a cheerful morning, though he had his usual view of the car park with its stationary cars and grey buildings in the background. He thought back to the night before and the view of the sea from the Landys' pool and thought there could not be two such contrasting experiences of Nairn.

He showered, shaved, and brewed coffee; he made it strong and dark. He wanted a sharp awakening of the brain; it was befuddled. He opened a kitchen cupboard, took out a packet of muesli, spooned some into a bowl, and added milk. He sat at the breakfast bar and switched on the TV.

His mind would keep on wandering back to the night before; he had some clear pictures of the others at that party and how much they had been enjoying themselves. He kept on seeing images of the guitar players and his mind lingered on the singer's voice; it had been pure and expressed emotions so well. People were laughing too loudly and making jokes then laughing again. Some were uncertain in their movements when they wandered around as the drink and drugs took effect.

He remembered thinking: no, don't jump in the pool after doing coke. But some did and splashed about and swam up and down. And jumped out. Then jumped in again.

Some of the memories were sharp and well-defined; others weren't. He grasped for them with his mind, but they slipped away. His head was aching, so he opened the drawer where he kept his aspirins and helped himself to a couple.

His mind hadn't focussed on the TV yet, which was a blur in the background. There was a news programme on, and the announcer was saying something about revenue figures. Then the picture switched to asylum seekers arriving on Dover beach. After the newsreader had droned on about that for a while, a picture of a pool appeared on the screen. What was it with pools? he thought. Then his mind took off again as a picture of Isla's face entered his mind. She had such a beautiful face, so young, so healthy, and carefree.

Then the TV programme caught his attention. The newsreader was saying something about a dead body floating in a pool, and something about a party, and the fact the body had been found with cocaine and alcohol in its system. The name of the dead person wasn't given as not all relatives had been informed, but the name of a famous actor, Mark Landy was. Jason wondered what he had to do with it. It was stressed the body wasn't that of Mark Landy and that Mark was nowhere near the party at the pool, but it was Mark Landy's pool. Jason's eyes were well focussed on the TV screen now, and, yes, that was the pool at Mark Landy's house in Nairn, and that was the lounger beside it that Jason had draped himself over the night before.

He gripped the arms of his chair as he tried to take this in. There was no picture of the body, but it was reported to be that of a young male. He thought of the young men who'd been at that pool party. Could it be Paul? He had seemed so healthy the night before – strong, muscular, tall, and full of vitality. Or could it be Andy – big, argumentative, in your face, Andy? Had there been an argument between him and Paul?

Something hovered at the edge of Jason's mind that he couldn't grasp. He tried to remember the things that had been said. Could it have been something about 'she's mine'? Or not? The memory of the voice broke up in his mind again. Hadn't there been an edge between Mark and Paul earlier? But Paul had been alive when Mark left his house for his plane. Then there had been the band. Had there been a disagreement with one of them – or between them?

A picture came to his mind of Andy diving into the pool with energy and he thought of the power in his crawl as he swam through the water. It was hard to believe any of them were dead. He wondered which one it was. It was a pity the programme had not said. How could one of them have died? All that life gone in an instant. The drugs of course; it must have been them. He'd pontificated in his mind that they shouldn't have been swimming after taking all that cocaine and alcohol, but he hadn't wanted to be right about that. Then he thought of Isla and wondered how she was coping with this.

FOUR

When the police turned up at Jason's flat, it was a shock, but he supposed they would be talking to everyone who was at that pool party. At least these policemen weren't high-ranking police officers, just a detective sergeant and a detective constable, but they had serious enough looks on their faces as they proffered their cards. Jason showed them in. When he saw them having a good look round, he found himself wishing the living room wasn't such a mess.

'I don't know them that well,' Jason said.

'You don't? You knew them well enough to be invited to their pool party.'

'I'd only just met Isla – at a café on the shore – when she invited me.'

'You must have impressed her.'

Jason thought there was something worryingly alert about the detective sergeant. He tried to remember the name on the card he had been shown and wished it hadn't been withdrawn so quickly after. Oh, yes. Ruthven. It had been a photograph of him too. Jason congratulated himself on being awake enough to notice that but thought that completely cognizant would be better. He felt at a disadvantage too because of his headache and that feeling of weakness in his limbs. Ruthven looked so clear-eyed, and physically fit; his skin seemed to glow. Jason wondered why his mouth had to be so dry and sticky; he had hardly been able to get any words out.

He offered Ruthven and colleague a seat – the constable's name hadn't stuck in his mind – but it was refused. They preferred to stand. Jason would have preferred it if they'd been seated. He slumped on a chair himself, feeling in need of the support.

'This won't take long, sir,' Ruthven was saying. That was reassuring at least.

'So, what happened?' Jason asked. 'How did he die? Who was it?'

Ruthven settled an authoritative look on him. 'In good time, sir. How well did you know the others at the party?'

'I'd only just met them.'

'How did they seem to you?'

'A bit drunk, which is what caused the problem I assume. I shouldn't think drink and pools mix.'

'Were there any arguments?'

Jason wondered why he was being asked that if they were investigating an accident.

'Not that I remember,' Jason said.

Not clearly anyway – despite the undercurrents. Should he mention them?

'Did you see drugs around?'

Jason wondered how to answer that. He didn't want to cause trouble for himself with the others at that party, nor did he want to get himself in trouble with the police by telling them lies.

'There might have been,' he said. 'Not that I take any myself.'

'Of course not, sir.'

Jason wondered at the sardonic tone in Ruthven's voice.

'So, I don't know what anything looks like but there was white powder being shared around. And it was being snorted.'

'Where did the drugs appear from?'

He wondered if he should tell them. Drug dealing is an offence. And he didn't like the expression on that sergeant's face. He had such hard eyes, the kind that would zero in easily on a lie. Jason told the truth. It wasn't as if he had been the one drug dealing. He had nothing to worry about – apart from revenge from the drug dealer.

'When the band arrived, that's when the drugs turned up.'

'The band?'

'Two guys and a girl. One of the guys was giving out packets of the powder.'

'Which one?'

'I don't know their names. He had a beard and a leather jacket.'

He told them everything he knew about the band, including some of the songs they'd been singing, and the fact they'd been good. He gave as detailed a description as he could.

'Thank you, sir,' Ruthven said. 'Don't worry about the names. We know who they are. You've been confirming what we already knew, which is useful. Thank you. What time did you arrive at the party?'

Jason told him.

'Can you describe everything that happened?'

Jason had a go at it, then had to confess his memory had blacked out after a certain point.

'That's unfortunate. So, you went back to your lounger after a couple of lengths, had a good gulp of your Manhattan, and that's the last thing you remember?'

More or less, Jason thought. He wasn't going to share what Isla had said to him about his smile. He didn't believe it had happened anyway.

'Could someone have put something in your Manhattan?'

'Anyone could if they'd wanted, I suppose,' Jason said. 'I did leave my glass by the lounger while I had my swim. Though why they would, I don't know.'

'Or it could have been the fact you'd had a few.'

'They were pretty strong.'

'You don't remember Paul having arguments with anyone?'

'Paul?' Jason said. 'Was it Paul who died?'

Ruthven didn't say anything, he just waited for Jason to answer his question, which he did.

'No. I don't remember Paul having a disagreement with anyone. I can't think who would argue with him. He was a great big, strong-looking guy.'

Was, Jason had said. He was sure it was Paul.

'And Paul seemed to be getting on with everyone?'

Now a picture conjured itself in his imagination of Paul lying face down in the pool, drifting, dead. And he'd been so alive.

'Yes,' Jason said.

'As you seem to have somehow worked out,' Ruthven said, 'it was Paul Robertson who died, not that there's any reason for it to be kept a secret now. His family have all been informed and it'll be in the papers soon enough.'

The police left shortly after that, leaving Jason with his emotions to deal with, and there were plenty of those. He couldn't believe that Paul was dead. He had seemed so alive the day before. And the police had been round at his house, asking their punctilious questions. There was a numbness in Jason. He had not taken everything in. How could he – so quickly?

A picture came to his mind, unbidden, and he wondered at it. It was of Andy glaring at Paul when Paul wasn't aware of him. Paul was talking to Isla at the time, and Jason wondered at the look. What had Andy been annoyed with Paul about?

FIVE

School the next day was interesting. After Jason had got out of his battered Mini in the car park, he found himself passing a couple of sixth-year pupils, which was usually met by a perfunctory but respectful 'Good morning, sir' accompanied by manufactured smiles. Today, their eyes goggled out of their heads, and they ducked out of speaking to him altogether, just rushed past, heads down. Jason supposed stories must be going around. He wondered how lurid they were. That new teacher was at a drugs-fuelled party, you know. He had something to do with that poolside death. Jason wondered how he was going to get through this.

When he entered the staff room, the first thing he noticed was the sudden quiet. Chatter was silenced when he walked in. Then voices started muttering reluctant greetings.

'Hi, Jason.'

'Hi, there.'

He gave a smile, said his good morning, then collapsed into a seat. There was some time till the bell for the first class, usually spent comparing notes with each other about the weekend. Now there were curious glances and a continued silence. Then it was broken.

'Good party?' one cheery voice called out.

'Good coke?' said another.

'It wasn't you dealing the stuff?' came from another direction.

Jason was simmering inside but managed a neutral reply.

'I don't do drugs.'

'Don't expect anyone to believe you,' said another voice.

'Lawson's going to kill you,' was called out cheerfully.

Jason thought he might now have properly announced his arrival at Rose High School. At least there was one note of envy.

'How on earth did you get to know Mark Landy?

It was the one remark Jason liked even though Mark Landy and he had probably exchanged about half a dozen words.

Before he could answer, a voice asked, 'How did that guy die anyway?'

But, of course, Jason would not just have a reputation for attending drugs parties, he was also now involved in a notorious death.

'I don't know much about it,' he said, 'just what you read in the papers. He was found floating in the pool. I don't know how he got there.'

Eric Sinclair was the person Jason knew best on the staff; he was a fellow English teacher, and, like him, in his twenties; unlike Jason, he was from Nairn, and Jason had valued his support, which Eric had given freely – until now. Jason noticed Eric was giving him a very strange look.

'Why on earth did you go? Those parties are infamous. Anyone with any sense would avoid them.'

'I hadn't heard about them,' Jason replied.

'I think you're in a world of your own half the time,' Eric said. 'How can you not have heard about those? Nice pool though, I'm told, and some cracking-looking girls. How did you even get the invite? You're sure it wasn't you delivering the coke?'

'I'm sure it wasn't.'

Jason was wondering what it was going to be like with the kids if this was how the staff were behaving. He began to dread his first class, 4A. He could see himself fielding questions all the way through the lesson. Then the staffroom door opened, and Lawson put his ginger head through.

'Sutherland. My office. Now.'

No beating about the bush there, and no time wasted once Jason was in Lawson's office either, surrounded by the multitudinous files and the pot plants, and feeling as menaced by them as by Lawson.

'What on earth did you think you were doing?' he said.

'Making friends,' Jason said. 'I didn't know what I was getting into. I didn't know there would be drugs there. And I certainly had no idea anybody was about to die from an overdose and hit the papers.'

'At Mark Landy's house. Have you any idea how much publicity this is causing?'

'I don't see how it can affect the school.'

'It won't. It could damage you.'

Jason was aghast at that. He hadn't had much to do with Dougie Lawson till then. He'd a long talk with Jason when he first arrived in order to welcome Jason to the school; and had given him a pep talk. Jason hadn't been especially worried by him, though he had noted Lawson wasn't someone he would want to fall foul of. But all heads were like that. Jason was studying him carefully now.

Dougie Lawson had short, cropped hair and a ginger beard. There were pronounced freckles on his face. He had long arms and legs, big, beefy hands, and a slightly mean-looking mouth. Jason hadn't noticed the sulky expression before. Perhaps that had just appeared. And Lawson's eyes were studying him in a way that reminded Jason of a frog being dissected in a laboratory.

'Are you facing charges?' Lawson asked.

'No.'

'The police didn't find drugs on you or anything?'

'I was clean as a whistle. I don't take the stuff so I would be. They asked me how I knew the Landys, and what happened at the party. They were asking background questions. Routine. That was the word they used. They were talking to anyone who was there.'

'It'll be interesting to see what the reaction of parents is. Of course, it's traditional to give staff full backing. But this is an unusual situation, and we need to see how it's going to pan out. I can't tell you to stay at home. I don't think so anyway. You say you didn't do anything wrong yourself. But if you want to take a couple of days off while we see how things are going to develop, I wouldn't be on your back for it.'

'That would make me look guilty of something,' Jason said. 'I need to carry on as usual.'

'It's a pity you see it that way. Are you sure you won't change your mind?'

'No.'

Lawson gazed long and hard at Jason. He tapped his fingers on his desk.

'I can't believe you've put me and the school in a position like this after we gave you a chance here. And you were in difficulties. You were lucky we hired you. Well, you're not getting to screw up my career. You've blotted your copybook big time whether you knew what you were getting into or not. And it's not three strikes and you're out here. It's one.'

Jason felt a chill in his blood now. How could he have had any idea what was going to go on at that party? Wasn't Lawson going over the top a bit here?

'When you're outside school, make sure you stay out of the public eye. Don't give interviews to newspapers. We'll field anyone who turns up at school. The real problem for you will be parents. They don't know you because you haven't been here long, though, on reflection, that may no bad thing. One or two of them enjoy causing a fuss. There's not enough going on in their own lives, so they try to look important round the school. This'll give them plenty to discuss with the School Board.'

Jason didn't know how Lawson usually ranted on, but it felt as if he was only getting warmed up. Fortunately, Lawson was nearly finished.

'If you really have made up your mind, you'd better go to your class, but are you sure you don't want to think about this again?'

There was one thing Jason was sure of at the end of the interview: if Lawson decided to relieve him of his classes, he would do so without hesitation.

* * *

After school, when Jason had dumped his briefcase and taken off his jacket in the haven of his flat, he slumped on the settee. What a day, and he had been right about 4A. The situation had been tailor-made for their sense of humour. And he had faced more sarcastic remarks as he moved around the school to teach his classes. And there were all those difficult silences and suspicious looks, and equally awkward moments with staff.

His head of department, Henry Kerr, was sympathetic. There was that plus point. He was critical of Lawson too.

'Tell me if you have any trouble with him,' he said. 'If I need to have a word with him, then I will do. From what you say, you've done nothing illegal. You were in the wrong place at the wrong time. He can't hang you for that, though I wouldn't put it past him to try. Watch out for him.'

Jason was grateful for that. Perhaps there was someone on his side, although Henry had also made Jason feel as if he was on a knife-edge. Jason had the feeling it would be easy to put a foot wrong and find himself in serious trouble, though he seemed to be in that already. He wished he had some way of predicting what behaviour on his part might make things worse.

His union rep gave bluff support. He was a teacher called Rob Edwards, who worked in the Maths department. He said if Jason had problems to make sure he involved him. He was entitled to support from his union rep. If Lawson decided to suspend him or give him any type of warning, there had to be notice of this, and the chance for him as union rep to help Jason prepare a defence.

'What defence do I need to come up with?' Jason asked.

'That depends on what the school decides to get up to,' he said.

That was no comfort and it bewildered Jason more than anything, so he was pleased to get to the end of that day and get the chance to hide in his flat. Overall, he thought everybody had seriously overreacted. All he'd done was attend a pool party, but he'd begun to wonder if Lawson's suggestion of a few days off would have been a good idea.

Jason's digital TV screen stood opposite where he was slouched, with its blank, black, and, at the moment, frightening face. He contemplated switching it on to brave one of the all-day news channels.

Instead, he took out his iPhone and scrolled onto the BBC News page. Perhaps it would be easier to view print. There was nothing on the national news page, so he scrolled onto Scottish news, and there it was, an article on what was now being called "The Poolside Murder".

Murder, Jason thought. That was the word they'd decided to use. The last time he'd seen the news, they'd been talking about a drugs overdose. Things had moved on. Jason wondered what had led them to decide it was murder. He read on. The skull had been fractured, most probably by a blow, with the post-mortem concluding that was the cause of death, not the drugs, nor drowning as there was no water in the lungs, indicating Paul had been dead when he entered the water.

Jason wondered how it could have happened. He started to think back to images that had presented themselves to his mind when he had woken up the day after the party. Had the raised voices been between Paul and Andy? Could he be sure about that? He had a clear picture in his mind of an angry Paul but no idea who he had been angry with. Then he found the courage to switch on his TV. There might be something more on live TV coverage.

There was a picture of an oil rig fire somewhere, which Jason looked at with curiosity. There was always something going wrong in the world. As long as it had been somewhere else, it had not unduly worried him, and he had never personally been connected with anything in the news before. That had changed, he thought, as the news picture switched to a scene at Mark Landy's house, and some print appeared on the bottom of the screen saying "Breaking News About The Poolside Murder".

Murder it was called in this coverage too; and things had moved on even since Jason had read the BBC News page on his iPhone. He watched agog as a newsreader, his voice full of the drama of his announcement, said that Isla Robertson Landy had been arrested in connection with the death of her husband, Paul Robertson. Then a picture of Isla appeared on the screen.

It was not a photograph of her being arrested; it looked as if it might have been taken from a social media page, and she appeared as he remembered her – pert, a bit overconfident, ready for whatever life might have in store for her. Jason did not suppose she looked like that now.

Jason's mind remained on her for some time. She was such an attractive young woman but what did he think of her really? He found himself wondering if she had murdered Paul.

He thought of her as she'd been at the party, talking to Lena and Amber. Lena was such a strange girl. There had been something unreal about her, someone in hiding behind a Marilyn Monroe act, but perhaps she was just an unsure sort of person who couldn't let her natural self be seen. Or was that the kind of nervous person who could end up killing someone? Jason knew nothing about these things, nor did he want to. She and Isla had been relaxed together – young women with laughter in their voices making the most of a fine evening. He had difficulty thinking either of them might have had anything to do with Paul's death.

And then there was Amber. She had seemed such an easy sort of person and when he'd seen her talking to Isla there had been a closeness between them, the kind there was between two people who understood each other well and who accepted each other. Isla had said Amber was always in part, an actress continually rehearsing, yet Jason had noticed none of that, just a slightly built young woman with an awkward kind of simper at times. No. Jason didn't think of her as a murderer.

And there was Joanne. There was a clear picture in Jason's mind of Joanne with her bright red hair and there had been a tension between her and Isla. He had noticed that. But she'd been relaxed enough with Paul. Or so he'd thought. There might have been a disguised awkwardness somewhere there.

And Ellie, the one with the big glasses and the expression on her face of someone who struggled to fit in and keep up. Could something there have erupted into violence?

Andy was the obvious suspect. There was something aggressive and over large about him that Jason could imagine easily turning to violence.

Jason didn't think Isla could have had anything to do with Paul's death, despite her arrest. She'd just been having a good night out as far as he could remember, and no one with a smile like that could be guilty of such a thing.

SIX

Jason was on a bench overlooking the firth opposite Nairn when he next met Isla Robertson Landy. He was contemplating the army of white waves rampaging over the firth, and the coolness of the sea breeze as it blew his hair everywhere. It was after school, and he'd been walking along the foreshore as a means of relaxing after the strains of a teaching day.

Things had settled down at school and there had been no alarming developments with parents or with Lawson, which he might have considered surprising as he was living in the middle of a lurid news story.

A figure seated itself beside him and he saw it was Isla. She wasn't anything like the self-confident, teasing, young woman he had first met. Her face held strain, and she had slumped onto the seat in a depressed attitude. But she was there, and he was glad to see her. She was no longer in the police station under arrest.

'They let you out,' Jason said.

'A couple of days ago,' she said. 'And thank God.'

'It's good to see you again,' Jason said.

'Likewise,' Isla replied, then became quiet.

With that intense look on her face, it was obvious the feelings she was experiencing were strong. Jason let her have her silence. It was little enough to allow given the situation she was in. Then a tear started to snake down her face, and she hauled a handkerchief out of her pocket and wiped it away.

'I'm sorry about what you've had to go through,' Jason said. 'It must be awful.'

'The police are pigs,' she said.

'I'm sure you're right,' Jason said.

'Honestly,' she said. 'It was bad enough losing Paul. Can you imagine what that was like? I was the one who found him, face down in the pool. It was awful. I didn't know what to do about it. I think I screamed a bit. Hollered the house down no doubt. Not that anyone paid attention. I didn't know where anyone had gone. Everyone seemed to have disappeared.'

'Yes,' Jason said. 'My memory's a bit vague about that night. I don't even remember going home.'

'You don't?'

'And the first I knew of what had happened at your house was when it appeared on the news. I couldn't believe it when I saw pictures of your pool. That was where I'd been the night before.'

'It was worse for us, believe me.'

She slumped further forward as she sank into silence.

'I think Johnny must have brought some bad stuff that time.'

'Johnny?'

'One of the band. I don't remember going to bed, just waking up there. And then, when I went downstairs and looked in the pool, there was my husband, lying there dead. Paul. He had his whole life ahead of him. Where's that gone? Paul? Dead? I still don't believe it.'

She put her hand up to her mouth and chewed a nail, which was unlike the cool, collected Isla he had first met. The last few days had reduced her.

She turned to look at Jason.

'Did you talk to him much?' she said.

'Not a lot,' Jason said. 'He didn't pay me much attention but then I'm not the most interesting person in the world. He seemed an OK guy. He did talk about his journalism and one or two of the people he'd met through interviewing them. I'll tell you one thing I did notice. He was very alive. He had a quick brain and, when he talked, it made it sound as if he was talking about the most interesting thing in the world to him. It's difficult to take in the fact he's dead.'

'Paul and talking. Yes. Paul could charm anyone. He usually did.'

She went quiet again as if something else had occurred to her that she did not want to remember.

Then she said, 'He charmed me anyway. To bits.'

She turned her head away as she sobbed.

Jason felt like holding her in his arms till those tears had the chance to dry up but, though they were close together on the bench, there was a distance between them that felt huge. The experience of finding her husband dead seemed to have taken Isla to a different place, a lonely one. And Jason had certainly never touched her before.

'Then the pigs arrest me. Me? As if I'd harm a hair on Paul's head. He was my husband. I loved him. You believe me, don't you?'

Her face turned towards Jason's, and he found himself looking into those violet eyes again, which were no longer lightly charming a room but burning through Jason with a pained intensity that hurt. They asked something of him that he felt compelled to give, whatever it was.

He put his arms around her and hugged her. She was close to him now, her head on his shoulder. Then she was sobbing again, and he was glad of the chance to hold her until those tears had stopped.

This was a beautiful and desirable young woman. Obviously, her father had good looks. He needed them in his job as an actor and he was successful at that, and Isla had inherited her own physical attractiveness from him. Now Jason had his arms around her.

That was an experience for a young man like him. He'd been feeling lost, alone, and sorry for himself, then suddenly he had a young woman like this in his arms. He didn't know what to make of it. He wasn't sure he knew how to cope with it, though he would do his best to help her through things and let her sob out her agony if she could.

Though the guilt he seemed to always carry with him since killing Eddie Caldwell rarely departed, he realised he had forgotten about it for at least five minutes. Isla had done that for him. He did not think he deserved this closeness with anyone, let alone with someone like her, but he held her tight.

'They were so sure I had something to do with his death,' Isla said. 'They asked all about my relationship with him. Did we still have sex? What fucking business is that of theirs? The nerve of it. I don't go up to complete strangers and ask questions like that. What right did they think they had to do that?'

'That does sound a bit much,' Jason said.

'And was I seeing anyone else? Why would I do that when I had Paul?'

'Quite,' Jason said, conscious his arms had just been around her, and sorry they weren't anymore.

'And was Paul seeing anyone? As if he would. We loved each other. We were married. Bloody police. What they think of people.'

'You're right,' Jason said.

Jason didn't feel there was much he could say. He supposed his role was one of respectful, sympathetic listener, and he did his best with that.

'And they asked what we'd been quarrelling about. Nothing, I said. We hadn't been. Apparently, somebody at that pool said we had. I'll kill them when I find them. Paul and I didn't have a cross word to say to each other all night.'

'How awful someone should say that,' Jason said. 'But the police believed you, didn't they? They let you go.'

'I don't know what they thought and what they didn't. I was just glad to get out of that police station. But they've gone off with my phone. And my computer. I don't know how I'm supposed to get on with anything without them. I hope they enjoy scrolling through that lot. There's nothing there.'

Then she went quiet again; she chewed another nail.

'Though they shouldn't be reading it.'

Jason wondered what it was she was thinking about. He certainly didn't like the thought of ever having to give up his phone and computer. Everything he did was recorded on them. The police didn't have the right to know that much about anyone.

'I'm free for the moment,' Isla said, 'but I'm still a suspect. They seem to think it's always the wife.'

'Have you any idea what happened at the pool?' Jason asked.

'No, is the short answer,' Isla said, 'except what the police have told me. Someone hit him over the back of the head and arranged him in the water to try to make it look as if he'd died of a drugs overdose.'

'Who might have done it?' Jason asked.

'God knows,' Isla said. 'They asked me all sorts of questions about that. Did he have any quarrels with anyone recently? they asked. Not at all. He was always charm itself.' She paused for a moment that seemed to last for a long time. 'But he was the cocky sort. If he wanted to have a go at someone, he did.' Then Isla became lost in thought for another long moment. 'And he and Andy had a ding-dong the other day. And I feel like a complete rat for telling the police about that. But what else could I do?'

'You were right,' Jason said, 'not that I've had experience of this sort of thing before. But I daresay you could be in trouble for withholding evidence. And somebody killed him obviously. Paul's dead. Could it have been Andy?'

'Absolutely no way,' Isla said. 'Not Andy.'

Jason regretted asking that question now. Those eyes were expressing fury with admirable clarity.

'And did I know who might want to kill him they asked. How would I know? Had anyone been threatening him? If they had, I'd have told them. The police are pigs. They ask their stupid questions without giving any thought to whether they're being hurtful or not.'

That was the third time Isla had described the police as pigs. They must have given her a torrid time.

'I expect there are questions they just have to ask,' Jason said.

Isla seemed calmer now. The expression of fury had disappeared, though there was still anxiety in her face, and she did have to keep chewing that nail.

'I wish they'd find out who did it.'

Then Isla started sobbing, and Jason found himself with his arms around her again.

'Hold me,' she said.

Jason did. He would have been glad to do that forever.

* * *

Jason started seeing Isla often after that. Fate can be odd, Jason thought. Who'd have thought they would ever have been brought together? They developed the habit of meeting up for lunch. It was a casual bite at another outdoor café along the shore. Jason had a box of fish bites and fries; Isla ate a vegetarian falafel. They sat on benches and enjoyed the fresh air and the peace. Jason learned more about Paul. Isla said he had played about with other women, and he had been a source of frustration to Isla about other things.

But she'd always loved him. She said she'd been obsessed with him. He had such a light air as if nothing mattered that much when you got down to it, so to hell with things, and get on and enjoy your life, why don't you? And that had appealed to her.

Isla said she had always been too serious, not that her father thought so, and Jason had to agree with him – that wasn't how he saw her. Isla said it wasn't easy being the daughter of a famous film star. Jason could only hazard a guess at that, so took her at her word. She said that was why she had always failed at everything. She had her Art degree but didn't seem to count that, nor the fact she taught Art. She had wondered about acting herself at one point, but her father had always warned her against it. He said it was no profession for a young woman because there was so much going on that shouldn't. She didn't want to have to sleep with anyone to get ahead, did she?

Jason had warmed to Isla from the first moment he'd seen her. Now he started to wonder if he was falling in love with her. He was fascinated by her, by the way she talked, by that so serious, faraway look in those eyes when she was speaking about something that mattered to her, by the way she jabbed her finger when she was making a point, by the sudden smile that would flash onto her face without warning.

Was she self-pitying? Jason might think that when he thought of some of the things she said – but there was a lot going wrong in her life. He didn't know anything about privileged backgrounds like hers and how helpful they really were. Did they cause difficulties? He liked the way she thought things through, and there was a spirit in her that appealed, and a young, healthy, animal magnetism. He did fancy her.

But Isla didn't seem to think of him that way. She was going through a difficult period and needed someone to talk to, and Jason felt the fact she'd singled him out for this was a privilege; a surprise too, but a good one.

She told him that Mark hadn't liked Paul, which was no surprise. The conversation Jason had witnessed between them at the pool had not been cordial. Mark thought of Paul as a dilettante; he'd told Isla from the beginning Paul was only interested in her because of who she was, Mark Landy's daughter, but Isla hadn't been convinced. She didn't think she was unattractive in herself. She'd pulled Paul, she was sure of it. But Mark was right in saying that Paul lacked ambition. The reason Paul got commissions for his journalism was because favours were called in by his family and friends. Attending expensive schools helped in that way, not that Paul appreciated it; he just accepted it as a right.

In time, Isla did admit she'd had a row with Paul on the night of the pool party, despite what she'd said at first. When she'd found out about a fling Paul was having, and with a friend of hers, she'd been furious, not that she told Jason who the friend was, which Jason wondered about. Isla was a bit like that. She behaved has if she was so forthright about everything, but there were things she only opened up about slowly.

Jason didn't mind. He liked listening when she spoke, to the musicality in her voice as much as anything; and watching her, the way emotions flitted across her face, the way she flicked her hair, and the way she crossed her legs as she sat on a bench.

He'd stopped feeling himself worthy of anybody since Eddie's death, not that he'd said such a thing to anyone. He'd supposed he should have taken to drink or drugs or something, but he hadn't learned to escape from things in those ways. Perhaps this was his escape from himself, listening to Isla and drinking in the vibrancy of her life, even though it was in chaos. But this wasn't going to end in romance. The mistake would be easy to make, but he knew enough about women to know that wasn't what these conversations were about.

He wondered if her father might have something to do with Paul's death but didn't say so. He thought Mark might have clashed with Paul and wondered if he should suggest the possibility to Isla. Fortunately, he realised that would be a bad idea. It would offend her, and he was enjoying Isla's company; he wasn't used to being the confidant of someone like her and didn't want to risk putting an end to it.

As the police had no developments to report to the press, publicity about The Poolside Murder began to die down. And they began to leave Isla alone, which was good.

This didn't stop Jason's mind mulling over things, often despite himself. Sometimes images from the party would appear in his mind. There was a picture of Joanne at one time, with her bright red hair and her clever teasing face, now turned sour as something annoyed her. That was different from what he'd remembered before, which worried him. Her mouth moved energetically as she expressed something urgent, though the voice remained elsewhere as did the words. Was this something his mind was creating as it played over the evening? The other person in that image was Paul, on the defensive, a bit puzzled and somewhat alarmed. Had there been something going on between Joanne and Paul?

SEVEN

When Jason walked into The Bandstand, the first person he saw was Andy, who'd arranged to meet him there.

The Bandstand was a public house and hotel that overlooked the Links on Nairn seafront. It also overlooked Nairn's bandstand, from which it took its name. This was a handsome, wrought-iron building with a gold-coloured cupola, which had stood there since Victorian days. It was not used by brass bands anymore but cut an attractive dash on the green and hence had survived, unlike a lot of the bandstands that had once graced small-town Scotland.

Andy looked serious as he propped himself up at the bar, drink on the counter in front of him while he contemplated the glass. He gave Jason a smile when he saw him. He had phoned Jason up and asked if he wanted to meet up for a drink, and Jason had said yes, not that he had any idea how Andy came to have his number. Someone must have given it to him, possibly Isla.

'Good of you to come over, Jason,' he said.

'Good to see you, Andy,' Jason said, though, if truth be told, as they had not spoken many words together before, Jason was more surprised to be there than anything.

Andy's reaction to him this time was different; it held a shade of the peremptory. There was something intimidating about Andy, even if Jason hadn't defined what it was. There was his size. He had several inches over Jason, a broad frame, and the look of someone who exercised regularly, but it wasn't just that. There was the confidence he exuded; there was an ease in the way he moved and expressed himself; and he had a firm jaw that might have graced a graphic novel character. He spoke with a well-paid-for accent, courtesy of Gordonstoun, and, underneath the public-school vowels, there was the suggestion of aggressive masculinity.

Andy held out his hand to shake Jason's with a grip that was just too firm. Jason rescued his fingers as soon as he could.

'What are you having?' Andy asked.

'What's that in your glass?' Jason asked.

'A Macallan,' Andy replied.

'That sounds good,' Jason said. 'I'll have the same if it's on offer.'

Andy turned and gestured to the barman.

'Another two of these,' he said.

The barman turned to oblige. Malt whiskies in front of them, they could relax, except there was something bothering Andy going by the frown on his face, and he didn't look as if he was unwinding.

'How are things?' Jason asked.

'Splendid,' he said, but scowled and turned his head away.

Then he looked back at Jason with a look of decisiveness on his face.

'Or as well as could be expected. I've had the police at me.'

'I'm sorry to hear it.'

'Which is why I wanted to meet up. We ought to get together, all of us who were there that night, and talk about things to see if it helps us make sense of it all. The police put some pressure on me. Have they had a go at you?'

'They talked to me briefly the day the body was discovered but I've heard nothing from them since.'

'Lucky you. Hope it stays that way for you. They seemed to think there was real aggro between me and Paul and I don't know where they got that idea from.'

'Not me,' Jason said. 'I don't remember much about that night. I was out of it. The Manhattans got to me. I don't even remember how I got home.'

'It wasn't memorable,' Andy said. 'Apart from the body they found the next day.'

Jason took a sip of Macallan. He wasn't sure what to say next. He wasn't going to let on that Isla had mentioned Andy's acrimonious conversation with Paul to the police. What was it Andy was expecting of him anyway? He didn't know. The image of Joanne had faded. Perhaps that had been imagination. Andy looked at the liquid in his glass. He seemed at a loss.

'I could kill them for the suggestion, of course, but not literally. Anyway, down to your problems.'

'My problems?' Jason said.

'You've been seen going around with the lovely Isla.'

'So?' Jason said.

'Do you think that's wise?'

'Why wouldn't it be?' Jason asked.

'You know, widow of the murdered man and you in an apparent relationship with her. What do you think it might look like to anyone with a suspicious mind – like your average policeman?'

Jason laughed, and it wasn't a light laugh. He was on the defensive, but he tried to force patience on himself.

'Look,' Andy said. 'I'm being serious.'

Jason took in the steely look in Andy's eye.

'You don't know what Isla's like at the moment,' Jason said. 'She's going through a lot. Anyone can see that. How do you think it's affected her? She's shattered – and worried sick. She needs someone to talk to.'

'And she hasn't any girl friends?' Andy said. 'She's got plenty, I can tell you. Why's she taken up with you?'

A good question, and one Jason had tried to ignore. It had been flattering that Isla had looked him out, and he liked being flattered – plus, she tugged at the heart strings. How could anyone not feel for Isla and want to help?

'And not only that,' Andy said. 'All of Isla's friends up to now have been ex-independent school like her.' He paused. 'With well-off parents as you would expect. One thing you could always say about Isla was that she stuck to her own class. So, why's she taken up with you?'

Jason ignored the implied insult in that.

'She needs to talk things through, and I can hardly say no,' Jason said.

Andy took a thoughtful sip of Macallan.

'You don't know her,' Andy said. 'You see her in this drama and that's all you know of her.'

He sighed.

'Don't become too fond of her. She picks people up and makes a fuss of them. Then she drops them when she feels like it. She makes use of people. She's using you.'

'So you say, but she needs someone to talk to. If she doesn't talk about things, she'll probably end up in some sort of nervous breakdown.'

'Is that what she's told you?'

'Of course not. It's common sense.'

Andy gave Jason a quizzical look. Then he continued with a note of gruff authority.

'About the party. Tell me your tale about that night.'

'Are you trying to get our stories straight for the police?'

'Just tell me what you remember.'

'A bunch of people lounged around, sipped Manhattans, and slipped in and out of the pool. What else would I have seen?'

'And the band?'

'It was a good band. I enjoyed their music. It was a pity about the drugs they brought with them.'

'Do you think so? You need to relax a bit, don't you?'

'Paul wouldn't have died if there hadn't been all that drug-taking going on.'

'You know that, do you?'

'It stands to reason.'

'Do you know how it happened – and who did it?'

'No.'

'Then how do you know it had anything to do with drugs?'

'Come on. Isn't that what it said in the newspaper? The body was found with cocaine in the system.'

'They also went on about a blow to the back of the head.'

'That doesn't mean there's no link to drugs,' Jason said.

Andy paused as he gave thought to what he was going to say next.

'So, you just saw people having a good time?' Andy said. 'There weren't any arguments going on?'

They were getting to what Jason couldn't quite remember, the memory of that voice shouting. If it hadn't been Joanne's or Isla's, he'd no idea who it belonged to. Could it have been Paul's? And what had it been saying? The voice disappeared from his head. If only he could remember things better. If only he could remember them at all.

'There was an argument then?' Jason said.

Andy gave him a glare in reply though Jason had no idea why the question would annoy him.

'As you said,' Andy replied, 'people were having a good time. So why are the police having a go at me?'

He knocked back his drink.

'All right. It wasn't you that told them,' he said. 'Now I've a man to meet.'

'Are you going already?' Jason said. It had been no time since he'd arrived, but Andy was striding away.

Jason realised he had found out nothing from Andy about the party, but that Andy had found out as much from him as he could, or as much as he thought he needed. Or he wouldn't be going off.

Then another image appeared in Jason's mind – limbs thrashing around. Where had that come from? He hadn't seen the murder – as far as he could remember. A picture of the body in the pool with blood seeping from it came into his head. Andy's face swam into his mind, Andy annoyed, Andy vicious, Andy swinging something and a scream. Jason had imagined that bit. It was too easy to reconstruct things according to his most recent theory. His mind was working too furiously on this. He had to keep separate what he was working out and what he remembered. It ought to be easy enough.

EIGHT

Jason hadn't a clue who could be ringing his doorbell at that time of night. It was eight o'clock in the evening. Not that anybody ever looked him up at any other time. He still hardly knew anybody in Nairn. When he opened the door, he found himself facing another two earnest-looking men bearing cards – and not Christmas ones. Jason had previously been relieved to be meeting only a sergeant and constable. This time the sergeant had brought along someone more senior.

'Good evening,' the newcomer said. 'I'm Detective Inspector Alistair Buchanan and this is Sergeant Andrew Ruthven – whom you've met. I'd like to ask some questions. May we come in?'

Jason didn't like the serious look in that tall, lean inspector's eyes but he didn't suppose he could refuse them entry. He ushered the two policemen into his small living room, where they seemed to take up an inordinate amount of room.

'Have a seat,' he said, as he took one himself.

It was the inspector he paid most attention to. He had another pair of alert eyes that darted about Jason's chaotic room where there was plenty for anyone to take exception to even if they weren't anywhere near OCD. The sergeant was the older of the two and seemed to take up twice as much room as the inspector, being broad as well as tall.

'We're still asking questions of everyone who was at that party,' Buchanan said, 'and establishing events.'

Jason noticed that Buchanan made no attempt to avoid making this sound intimidating, and he duly quaked.

'Sorry I wasn't more helpful before,' Jason said. 'My memory of it isn't clear.'

'A pity,' Buchanan said, and Jason could see his brows knit together.

The inspector waited as if expecting him to continue, which he didn't. He had no idea what to say.

'No one else at that party has a memory lapse like yours,' Buchanan said.

'I'm not good with alcohol,' Jason said.

'And nobody remembers you having any more to drink than anyone else.'

That was pointed and put Jason on the defensive.

'I don't drink much,' Jason said. 'Perhaps those strong cocktails affected me more.'

That was probably true. Jason didn't drink at all at parties if he could help it. He liked to be aware of everything around him, didn't fancy the idea of a headache the next day, and alcohol made him feel sleepy. He still wasn't sure why he'd accepted those Manhattans. Something to do with Isla, with the house, and the fact it was a pool party at the house of a famous actor? Had he just fallen asleep that evening?

'So, tell me what you do remember.'

Jason repeated what he had said before. It was best to stick to that and not confuse things.

'Can you tell me anything about the argument between Paul and Andy?'

The argument Andy had been talking about with Jason – and denying – but it did fit in with Jason's initial vague memory of angry voices.

What he said was, 'Not really.'

Now the sergeant spoke.

'Not really? What does that mean?'

Jason tried to take this in. The inspector didn't look as if he needed a partner to make sure the witness cooperated but perhaps that was supposed to be the sergeant's job.

'My memories of that night are vague,' Jason said. 'Which is an understatement. But I have some sort of recollection there were raised voices, not that I could tell you any more than that. It's all...' Jason spread his arms vaguely to indicate helplessness about this.

'You didn't say anything about raised voices before.'

That was the sergeant again.

'What is there I can say?' Jason said. 'I didn't think there was anything I remembered that could be useful to you. Sorry.'

'Are you sure there's nothing else comes to mind?' Buchanan asked.

'There's nothing else,' Jason said.

'You couldn't think a bit harder about what you remember about the raised voices?'

'I've tried,' Jason said. 'It doesn't help.'

'Do you want to be charged with withholding evidence?'

That sounded heavy to Jason. Why was the inspector taking that approach? But Jason thought it wise not to argue.

'I definitely don't,' he said.

'But you must remember something else,' Buchanan said.

Jason struggled to recollect anything at all now.

'There's nothing clear,' he said.

'But something?'

Jason thought about it, but the more he did that, the less clear anything seemed. He spread his arms helplessly again.

'Was it a male angry voice?'

'It might have been.'

'Might have been?'

For some reason an image of Amber came to him, looking shrewish and making a pointed comment. How many people at the party had he imagined having an argument with Paul now?

'I think it was, yes.'

He was sure it hadn't been Amber's voice. Yes. He was.

'Young or old?'

'I don't know. Look–' But then Jason realised he did. 'Young. Yes. It was a young voice.'

'Accent?'

But the voice slipped away again.

'I don't remember the words, never mind the accent.'

'You can't remember anything he said?'

'No.'

Buchanan frowned.

'You said voices. What can you tell me about the other voice? Was that male as well?'

'Did I say voices?'

'Yes.'

Jason did his best to concentrate but nothing clear emerged.

'I only really remember the one,' he said. 'I assumed he was arguing with someone. And I'm very sorry about this. That's the last time I say yes to a Manhattan.'

The inspector allowed his face to relax slightly. He had come to the end of that line of questioning.

'It's a pity you don't remember more, but if anything does come back to you, and it probably will, be sure to be in touch.'

'Yes,' Jason said. 'But…'

'But what?'

'If I think I remember any more now, can I trust it? Can I be sure I'm remembering things properly? I don't want to give the wrong impression about anybody.'

'We wouldn't want that. Still, you could remember more.'

'Maybe,' Jason said. 'I don't know.'

Jason didn't. Nor did he want to remember anything clearly. He didn't want the responsibility that would go along with that.

'You say you hardly knew anyone there?'

The frown had reappeared on the inspector's face. There was something else he wanted to work away at with his questions.

'Yes,' Jason said.

'We did check up on that, which is why you haven't figured much in the inquiry. You sounded from the initial interview to be–' he paused as he gave thought to his words '–an accidental presence. And we had a lot of things to investigate. But we've since discovered you have a relationship with the wife of the murdered man.'

Andy had warned Jason that was a bad idea.

'Only since the party,' Jason said. 'Give me a break here. She's cut up about the whole thing and looking for people to talk to. I was there. Why wouldn't she talk to me about it?'

'And now our attention has been drawn to you, we've found out more about you.'

Oh, Jason thought.

'We do know about it.'

Oh.

'You killed a man.'

That little matter.

Involuntary Act Culpable Homicide was the technical term for the conclusion the court had come to on his case, which is manslaughter in England. Whatever it was termed did not matter that much to Jason. He had killed someone, even if he had been admonished.

'That was gone through thoroughly at the time,' Jason said to Inspector Buchanan.

'Obviously,' he said. 'And we've read up on it. I want to hear it in your words.'

Jason did not want to talk about that, as might be expected. As the judge and jury were convinced by his solicitor's plea, Jason had escaped a prison sentence, though that did not make him feel any less guilty and he did not want any of that dragged up again. But this stern-eyed inspector would have it out of him, he could tell.

He couldn't complain; he had killed someone and deserved every ounce of suspicion from the man in front of him. As far as Jason was concerned, whatever the arguments put forward, it had been murder. After all, it hadn't even been easy to establish that the Culpable Homicide was involuntary. He'd only managed it by telling that important white lie, so he would have to be careful how he answered these questions from Buchanan. He'd never had any regrets about Eddie Caldwell's head hitting that marble tabletop, though that had been accidental. He had been defending his girlfriend, but his lack of remorse at killing a man had surprised him. He was still unable to get used to the idea of that part of himself, but he was glad he knew better than to admit any of this to a policeman investigating another death in his vicinity.

'It was an accident,' Jason said.

'You swung a punch by accident?' the inspector said.

'No. Obviously,' Jason said. 'Look. You don't know how it was.'

As the inspector waited for Jason to explain that, Jason found himself starting to go through it in his head again, everything that had happened that dreadful evening.

'He raped her,' Jason said.

'In a pub in front of everyone?' Buchanan asked.

'No.'

Jason finished gathering his thoughts.

'Eddie was in a relationship with Renée, my girlfriend – before I knew her. He'd never stopped resenting the fact she'd finished with him.'

'Go on.'

'He was a controlling person, and Renée tired of that. He put a device on her phone to track her, for heaven's sake. She told him where to go. He told her she was his and there was no way he was letting go of her, which was when he raped her. When she complained to the police, it didn't help at all. She'd been in a consensual relationship with him, and it was only her word against his, which made it impossible to prove rape. And she'd had a bath afterwards because she'd felt the need to be clean after what he'd done to her, so there wasn't even physical evidence of anything.

'At least he got some sort of message from the fact she went to the police. He left her alone for a while, but not for good. He started texting again later – and stalking her. He threatened to kill me because I was seeing her. The reason he turned up at that pub was he'd followed us there. He said it was time to have it out. She was his and she was leaving there with him. He tried to haul her after him. I pulled back at his arm. He pulled away. I pulled back again. I just wanted him to get his hands off Renée. Unfortunately, in the scuffle, he fell over a bar stool and hit his head on something as he fell. I was only trying to stop him. I didn't mean to kill him.'

'He fell over a bar stool?' Buchanan said. 'And the jury bought that?'

'It's what happened. There were enough witnesses there. It happened in a pub.'

It had been a relief to Jason that witnesses had taken his side. It must have all happened so quickly they hadn't a proper sight of what had happened. Oh, yes, all Jason had done was pull at Eddie, but he had judiciously positioned his own leg so that he could lever Eddie off balance as he pulled at him. It had been luck that stool had fallen at the same time. He'd never admitted any of this, even to his lawyer, because he had the feeling if it had come out, he wouldn't have escaped a jail sentence.

Jason's words had run out and he was left feeling drained. He gaped at Buchanan as he watched his reaction. From the beginning of Jason's speech to the end, the expression on Buchanan's face had remained the same, one of furious concentration. While Jason had been stumbling through everything, Buchanan had been working out whether he believed what Jason was saying, and what kind of person all of this made him.

'You were lucky to get your verdict,' Buchanan said, 'not that it sounds as if you did intend to kill him. But it would have been easy for them to see it differently.'

Jason heaved a sigh of relief. He'd been admonished again.

NINE

When Isla had phoned up to arrange lunch, she had sounded desperate, and Jason couldn't say no when there was that note in her voice. So, there they were sitting on Nairn foreshore again on a wooden bench, paper coffee cups beside them. Was it glamour that had attracted him to Isla? They certainly didn't meet in glamorous places. She did carry a Louis Vuitton bag and the rings on her fingers were gold with glittery stones; she came from a different world, but she inhabited this one; like him, she was happy to sit with a cardboard carton in her hands as she had lunch, and there was a fresh scuff mark on her shoes.

The first thing she asked was if the police had been round to ask him about the murder, which was the obvious question, but he wasn't prepared for it. He decided to say no because it hadn't been that death they'd spent so much time asking him about and he didn't want to alarm her.

'Lucky you,' she said. 'They've been questioning me again. And they've been asking about my relationship with you. You're sure they haven't been to see you?'

As Jason stuck to his lie, he thought it was a pity he had to; he was not enjoying lying to Isla.

'Expect them at some point,' she said.

'OK,' Jason said.

She gave him a pitying look.

'They drove me frantic when they came round,' she said.

Jason hated hearing that.

'I suggested the obvious line of inquiry to them, but they just suit themselves.'

'Obvious line of inquiry?' Jason said.

He hadn't realised there was one.

'Don't you think it's easy to work out who they should be questioning?'

'Not from where I'm sitting.'

'Joanne, don't you think?'

Joanne? Jason thought.

'Joanne Muirhead. She's the one who was having an affair with my husband.'

'She was?'

'You didn't know? I thought I'd told you.'

Yes, for all that directness of Isla's, the truth trickled out of her slowly. It was odd that it coincided with something that had occurred to Jason before.

'No. I suppose I didn't. It was Joanne he was seeing this time. I was furious with her. She was my friend. And she did that to me? What kind of friend is that?'

That did fit in with some of the things that had been going through Jason's head. Perhaps they hadn't been so crazy after all.

Isla picked at her falafel and stared out to sea with a venomous expression as he thought about things some more. Isla had described a complicated relationship with

Paul, but he didn't see how that gave Joanne motivation to kill him.

'I think she'd fallen for him big time but there was no way he would have left me.'

He wouldn't? Jason thought. He wondered how Isla knew that.

'He always came back to me. Paul lived for the moment, and he did have the brief occasional affair, but it was me he was committed to.'

'If he saw others on the side, wouldn't you have been happier if he'd left you for one of them? You can't have liked it when he was unfaithful to you.'

'It was who he was. You hardly knew him. You don't get him.'

Jason gave her a puzzled look.

'He had to have his freedom. It was what made him the person he was.'

That just sounded – Jason wasn't sure how to put it – naïve on Isla's part. But apparently it was very Isla. Perhaps it was something to respect. Isla was someone who accepted people as she found them instead of trying to make them into something else. There was one thing for sure, and that was he had never met anyone like her.

'Joanne was serious about people. She wouldn't understand someone like Paul. He was wrong for her. Right for me.'

Isla gave a giggle, which jarred. Possibly it was some kind of semi-hysteria.

'I can believe she killed him in an argument. And the police don't suspect her at all. It's always the husband or wife that does it. Isn't that what they say in crime TV dramas?'

Isla's face puckered up. She was attempting to resist tears and it made her look… well, any expression on her face made her look beautiful to Jason – and he wanted to put his arms round her again and protect her.

'I miss him,' she said. 'There was so much life in Paul. How can he be dead?'

'It's all tragic,' Jason said. 'Unbelievable too. I haven't taken it in yet either.'

Then Isla did burst into tears and Jason found himself with his arms round her again.

He and Isla sat together in silence for a while. Jason had no experience of helping someone through something like this, but he held her, and, in the end, she became calmer, if no happier.

'I did think of killing myself,' she said.

'No. Don't do that.'

'The police couldn't harass me then.'

'Can't your father do something about them?'

'The police are allowed to ask questions,' Isla said. 'It's their job.'

'I suppose,' Jason said. 'But you obviously didn't murder Paul. They're bound to give up questioning you in the end.'

'I have read how to do it,' Isla said. 'All you do is sit in your car with the engine running and the garage doors closed. You fall asleep. And then you don't wake up.'

'That wouldn't give things a chance to change for the better. Does your father know you have thoughts like these?'

'No. And don't you dare tell him. What difference would it make anyway?'

'Have you talked to a doctor about it?'

Then something approaching a smirk appeared on Isla's face as if she was enjoying the sympathy. That was a bit self-indulgent, Jason thought, although, as she was going through such hell, he shouldn't criticise.

'How could a doctor help?' she said.

She gave him a piercing look.

'Words. Words. Words,' she said. 'A smorgasbord of words. Cheer up, Jason. I'm letting my feelings out. That's all.'

Then she gave him one of her more devastating smiles, and Jason hoped it was as she'd just said because he'd fallen for her, hook, line, and sinker.

* * *

So, he was pleased when he next received a text from her asking him over to the posh eco-house. To his surprise, Mark Landy answered the door.

'Hi', he grinned.

'Oh, hi.'

Jason tried not to behave like a startled rabbit. He had only talked to Mark Landy once before – and that had been brief.

'Come in,' Mark said. 'Isla's upstairs just now. If you come into the living room and wait, she'll be down soon.'

Jason found himself in another room that was the whitest of white – with a yellow and black Jackson Pollock on the wall and a view out to sea and sky. Was that a real Jackson Pollock? As Jason seated himself on the edge of a settee, he tried hard not to stare at it, though perhaps that might be allowed. That was what works of art were for, after all. Jason tried to look relaxed. Mark seated himself opposite, where he looked at ease – as he should, Jason thought. It was his own home. Mark was still grinning as he studied Jason.

'You've become quite the friend of Isla's,' he said.

'She seems to need someone,' Jason replied.

'I think she does,' Mark said.

He studied Jason, which felt uncomfortable. Jason didn't think of pointing out to Mark Landy he might be staring, and Jason was about to look away when Mark started to speak.

'Yes. You do look like him. Very.'

'Who?' Jason said.

It hadn't occurred to him he looked like anyone in the Landy entourage.

'Leslie, Isla's cousin. They were very close. I suppose that's why she can talk to you so easily.'

'I didn't know about Leslie.'

'There's no reason why you should. And I ought to say thank you, by the way.'

'You ought to?'

'Yes. You've been doing Isla a lot of good. Paul's death – as you might expect, it's shattered her. And that attention from the police! That was inexcusable. I made sure I had my lawyers at them for that. The police haven't been bothering you, have they?'

'Not lately,' Jason lied.

He seemed to be getting on well with Mark Landy, famous actor that he was, and he didn't want to spoil things by confessing the police had been grilling him about someone he had killed in the past.

'I'm glad to hear it. They were over the top at Isla. I suppose it made sense to them. My solicitor has made it clear to them to leave her alone unless they have something approaching evidence, which they don't, and couldn't possibly have – obviously. This taking her into the police station on speculation isn't on. We'll sue them for harassment if they're not careful.'

Then Mark stopped rattling on and looked at Jason in a way Jason couldn't quite decipher. Or was that relief on Mark's face?

'But it's done her a lot of good to be able to talk to you. Really, it has.'

'I'm glad to hear it,' Jason said. 'She needs someone to listen to her. Anyone would under these circumstances.'

'Quite. As I said, she really was close to her cousin. He was like a brother to her, which is how she sees you, I think. She always wanted a brother.'

Is that it? Jason thought. Brother. Ah well.

'And she's fragile.'

'Is she?'

'Oh, yes. As a teenager she really lacked confidence. We had her join all sorts of groups to try to cure that. Improvised drama. The debating club at school. You probably wouldn't think it now.'

Mark paused again as he waited for an answer.

'You'd think the opposite,' Jason said.

'Yes. I know. We're proud of the way she's turned out. But she had to be taught all that, you know. Look the person you're talking to in the eye. Smile. And she has a lot of poise now. But underneath that she's still a bit of a delicate flower.'

'I see.'

This did explain something about Isla. All that studied insouciance was a role she played, even if she did it so well.

'I'm glad she has someone she can talk to about this. You're non-judgemental, and that does her a lot of good.'

'I'm glad to hear it.'

'I wanted to say thank you.'

'It's a pleasure,' Jason said.

'When her cousin died, she was inconsolable,' Mark said.

'I didn't know about that.'

'He fell into a weir. He was supposed to be meeting up with Isla that day, but he didn't turn up. It was days later when they found his body. He had drowned. Death by misadventure it was called. He was a good swimmer but there had been a lot of rain and the river was heavy and too much for him. It was dreadful. His parents had such hopes for him too. He was a talented boy.

'Isla fell apart. She needed medication, treatment. We thought she might have to go through all that again after Paul's death. But she's coping. Which is great. You seem to have saved the day. What can I say? Thanks again.'

'I'm sorry to hear about her cousin,' Jason said.

And Jason was. What a horrible thing to happen, and perhaps it explained something about Isla that had puzzled him, that surprising clinginess she had.

'She's easily hurt, Isla. She's such an emotional person. We always had to be so careful with her. Lily is too. Not that she and Isla have really hit it off. So, Lily keeps her distance and allows Isla the space she needs to be herself.'

He gave Jason another thoughtful look.

'So, you be careful with her too.'

'I will be,' Jason said, and he meant it. Isla had become meaningful to him.

That was when Isla walked in, gave Jason a dazzling smile and Mark an anxious stare.

'I've been making him welcome,' Mark said.

'Are you sure you haven't been scaring him away?'

'Not guilty,' Mark said.

'Because you've scared friends away before.'

'Not good ones,' Mark said.

'I'm glad you think he qualifies as that. There's no harm in Jason.'

Mark nodded.

'I'll leave you two together,' Mark said. 'I've a script to study.'

Then Mark disappeared somewhere, and Jason tried to come to terms with that conversation as he asked Isla how she was, and they settled down to chat.

TEN

Jason had a spare period in the fourth lesson every Monday when he would slump on a chair in the staffroom, drink coffee, and chat to anyone who happened to be around. The opportunity not to think about anything apart from mindless chatter was to be grasped at after the amount of concentration needed to teach a class. He had to be so aware of everything that was going on in the class as well as attempt to deliver a learning experience.

Eric was there as usual, Eric, who had been such a patient mentor when Jason had first arrived, but who was now looking at him as if he was some sort of pariah.

'Is everything OK?' Jason asked.

'In my life,' Eric said, then lapsed into silence.

Jason tried to work that out.

'Have you any idea what you're doing?' Eric said.

Jason's mind was still trying to untangle itself from 4A, whom he thought he'd been teaching well that morning. He had the impression they'd understood something of Macbeth, and even the wayward Allie McPhail had been quiet.

'What do you mean?' Jason said. 'My classes are going OK, as far as I know. How are yours?'

'That's not what I meant. Though it remains to be seen how long that will last given the impression you're creating.'

Jason looked at him with puzzlement. He had been trundling along reasonably steadily with things, hadn't he? Nothing was different from usual.

'She's a stunner. I can see the attraction.'

He meant Isla, Jason thought. He'd dismissed Andy's warnings about pursuing a relationship with her some time ago, but now he was being lectured about it by someone else and it was alarming.

'Isla, you mean?' he said. 'There's nothing in it. We're friends, that's all. A teacher is allowed to have those.'

'You live in Nairn. Have you any idea how many of our parents live there too? And have you any idea how quickly gossip goes round somewhere the size of Nairn?'

Jason didn't want to accept this, but he had no idea how to reply to it.

'Do you know what they're saying?' Eric continued.

'Who?'

'Everyone.'

Jason's mind blanked at that. He couldn't take in the concept of everyone. Eric must mean particular people, if not just the one.

'Who's saying what about me?'

'You're trying to tell me you haven't any idea?'

'About what? Come on. Out with it. Tell me exactly what you mean.'

'The gossip – and I mean with pupils, parents, and amongst fellow staff – is that you're in a relationship with Isla Robertson and the fact you're so blatant about it so soon after her husband's death means you must have been having an affair with her for some time before he died too.'

Then he paused – for dramatic effect, Jason supposed. Eric did teach drama. His school play, not that Jason had seen it yet, was supposed to be spectacular. Though Jason didn't want to know any more about this performance.

'Gossip's so much better than real life, don't you think?' Jason replied. 'Much more interesting.'

'At least you feign some sort of innocence,' Eric said. 'But I wouldn't dismiss talk. You're a teacher. It can matter.'

'I'm not doing anything wrong,' Jason said. 'Isla's devastated by her husband's death. She needs anyone she can find to talk to.'

'I can see why you're flattered,' Eric said. 'Her father's famous. She's rich. And an absolute cracker. That could go to anyone's head. But don't you see how dangerous she is for you?'

A picture of Isla came to his mind, the happy, laughing Isla he had met briefly before the poolside incident. That was followed by another image: the tearful Isla putting her head on his shoulder. Neither seemed dangerous to him.

'Have you no sympathy for other people?' Jason said. 'She needs a shoulder to cry on. You've no idea what she's going through. So, there's mindless prattle from people

71

who should know better. I don't see why I should pay any attention to that.'

'Someone murdered her husband. And people are saying it was you.'

That struck Jason as silly. He'd barely exchanged more than a few words with Paul. No one could reasonably suppose he might have killed him.

Eric continued.

'Let me put this simply so that anyone could understand – even you. People are saying you have been having an affair with Isla and that you killed her husband so that you could have her. After all, it's you she's hanging around with so soon after his murder. It makes sense.'

Jason was speechless at first. Then words tumbled out with great indignation.

'I'd barely met her when Paul was found dead.'

'That's not how it looks. And it's not what people are saying.'

That disconcerted Jason but, when he thought back to 4A, their mood had been odd. They'd made quiet progress with Macbeth, but they'd been subdued. They hadn't been so much showing interest in the text as avoiding interaction with him. There had been no enthusiasm, and there had been unruliness in some of those glances; and silences where there would have been silly chatter. Perhaps they were starting to see him as a sort of Macbeth.

'You think I should drop her because of gossip?' Jason said.

'It would protect you. It would be sensible.'

He thought back to Isla; she was so vulnerable and needy. He didn't want to let her down.

'You're from Edinburgh,' Eric said. 'Perhaps you don't understand small towns.'

He'd always thought of Edinburgh as being a bit of one of those itself, but he supposed Eric was right.

'Small-town life,' Eric went on. 'There's gossip about everyone. Or most people. Sometimes it feels as if you only need to walk out of the door for someone to make up something about you. Maybe it's the short days in winter up here. People have nothing to do but make up stories about each other.'

'And nothing to be done about that any time soon,' Jason said. 'But that won't stop me getting on with my life.'

'You do need to be careful about how you behave when there's all this talk going around about you. It's probably just started.'

'You're telling me to stop seeing Isla,' Jason said.

'That's what I've been saying.' Eric's voice was no longer stern. He was speaking as one friend to another and there was kindness there. Jason wondered if he should pay attention to him.

'It's ridiculous,' Jason said. 'I'd only just met Paul – and Isla – before that murder happened.' He wondered how many more times he was going to have to say that. 'I had nothing to do with it and I don't see why I should have to act like a guilty person. That wouldn't help the rumours. It would make them worse.'

'So, you've made up your mind,' Eric said.

'Definitely,' Jason said.

* * *

Dougie Lawson had summoned Jason to his office again and Jason found himself sitting in front of his headmaster's desk, gazing at the picture behind it and wondering what it was. It was Dougie Lawson's idea of modern art. Jason had worked out that much. His attempt at culture looked like an inkblot to Jason. Perhaps it was one, though why it had been framed was beyond Jason. The serious look on Lawson's face that morning made Jason feel like a blot on the landscape himself. He resisted the desire to squirm and affected a puzzled look – though that didn't have any positive effect on Lawson. Jason thought later that nothing would have done.

Jason had heard it said red-headed people have short tempers. He knew this was belied by Dougie Lawson who was in possession of an extremely controlled persona though something about his red-haired countenance did convey displeasure clearly. Not that he seemed to know how to phrase anything at first, just staring at Jason from behind his desk. He made one attempt to start, changed his mind, stood up, looked out of his window, then returned to his seat and frowned at Jason instead.

Jason didn't know him well enough to know if this was partly an act designed to unsettle him, but something was causing Lawson concern and Jason found that worrying. Then Lawson started drumming his fingers on his desk and that made Jason even more nervous.

'Look, Jason, this is difficult.'

'Yes, sir.'

Jason supposed he had a bemused expression on his face by now.

'Normally when I tell teachers to come into my office, it's because of a particular incident, and there hasn't been one. You avoid those well. You're good with your classes. You skate round potential problems. And, on the whole, they enjoy your teaching. So, this makes me feel guilty.'

'Yes, sir?'

'I've had a lot of parents coming up to me with concerns.'

'No one's said anything to me.'

'That may be part of the problem. If they had a better line of communication with you it might help. But what it is, is…' He drummed his fingers on the desk again. 'They don't fault your work with their children. They wonder if you're a murderer or not.'

Jason was aghast at that.

'But that– sir– you can't be taking that seriously. I object.'

'I don't think you've murdered anyone, but they do. They wonder if you murdered Paul Robertson.'

'Tell them to go take a running jump. It's ridiculous – and slander. Shouldn't you be protecting me instead of listening to them and bringing it up with me?'

'I do tell them I don't believe it.'

'Thanks for that.'

'But I did tell you before that there might be a parental reaction to your being involved in that poolside incident. How do we deal with it as a school?'

'I wasn't involved in it. I was just there the evening it happened.'

'You've told me that and I don't disbelieve you. But it's possible some of them could tell their children not to attend your classes. That has been discussed amongst them.'

'Can they do that?'

'You need to be careful with parents, Jason. You don't want them taking against you, which is what they're doing.'

Jason was furious – with the parents obviously, but with Lawson also. Shouldn't he be doing a better job than this of protecting someone on his staff?

'So, what can I do about it?'

'Can I ask you a question?'

'What?'

'Did you do it?'

'Of course I didn't,' Jason said.

Jason could feel himself beginning to lose patience. Perhaps it was a wonder he hadn't before this. He cautioned stoicism on himself. Lawson had been asking the obvious question.

'Perhaps if you didn't make yourself look guilty it would help. You're in a relationship with Isla Robertson. Everyone knows that.'

'It depends on what you mean by a relationship. We're friends. That's all. She needs someone to talk to. You would as well if your nearest and dearest had just been murdered. I think some of our parents need to get a life instead of sitting in judgement on their children's teachers so much. I'm trying to teach their kids. That's all.'

'And you're doing it well. But, Jason, if their parents think you might be a murderer, so do your pupils. It can't be comfortable for them. Don't you think?'

'I know I didn't do it. And I resent being accused of it.'

'Could you stop seeing this Isla – so publicly at least?'

'What?'

'You're meeting her on Nairn seafront, for heaven's sake. Everyone goes there.'

'I'm not sure you should be interfering with my private life.'

'But it affects your teaching.'

'I teach my classes well.'

'I don't doubt your abilities, but this is bound to affect your performance.'

Jason could think of no more to say in his defence for the moment. Lawson had intimidated him into silence, which he did have a reputation for being able to do. Jason admired his style. He'd done it well.

'I do feel for you. It must be dreadful to walk accidentally into a situation like this where you haven't – technically – done anything wrong.'

And thank God Lawson thought that, though Jason wished he hadn't modified it by saying 'technically'.

'Which is why I'm not going to do anything at all. I'm hoping it will blow over.'

That would be good, Jason thought.

'If I suspend you, it'll look bad for you.'

'Yes, sir.'

'I don't want to make things look worse for the school either. It's tittle-tattle. I've listened to a lot of that from parents before this and it often is unfair and ill-considered. It can also get seriously out of hand, which might not do me any good if I continue to do nothing.'

He sat back in his chair and gave a sigh, a deliberate one.

'I did you a favour by giving you this job. I know we desperately needed someone at the time as we'd just lost someone halfway through the year, but all the same, there were serious arguments against you.'

Oh, those, Jason thought.

'You don't have to declare Involuntary Culpable Homicide when you apply for employment. I do realise that. But still, this is an independent school that takes great pride in itself, and the only reason we ignored it was because of influence. Your solicitor of the time has links with the board – and he felt sorry for you. You must have made a good impression with him.'

Jason had been surprised at this job offer at the time and grateful for it. He had been very low after the court case.

'The least you could have done was take advantage of the opportunity. I must tell you that you're throwing your life away – again.'

'But–' Jason started to speak then thought better of it.

'The only advice I can give you is to try to avoid gossip. The fact you live in Nairn is a problem because so many of our parents live there too. It would be easier if you stayed elsewhere, not that I should be telling you where to stay.'

He gave another large sigh and this one sounded even more heartfelt.

'And we'd better leave it at that,' he said.

* * *

Jason had always avoided social media. He'd thought that, if he had no accounts, he wouldn't find himself discussed on them, and perhaps it had helped. His court case hadn't become generally known in Nairn, but he'd become a Twitter star now. He'd discovered that when 4A told him.

'You must be good in a fight yourself, sir.'

They were at a lurid point in Macbeth. Macbeth was preparing for battle, and, as Jason's thoughts were on the text and his interpretation of it, he wasn't ready for war in the present day.

'What do you mean?' he said.

'Everyone knows all about it.'

Jason's interlocutor was Allie McPhail, jackass extraordinaire, born comic and entertainer, and leader of all class tomfoolery – when he could get away with it. Jason gave him an appraising look but did not reply.

'It's all over the internet,' Allie said.

'What is?'

'You killed Eddie Caldwell,' he said. 'Everybody knows about that now. You were up for it in court. So, what are you doing here teaching us?'

'I–' Jason said, then stopped.

Jason was dumbfounded. His brain seemed to have seized up with the horror of this.

'I was admonished,' he said. 'It was accidental.'

'That was lucky for you, sir. Wasn't it?' Allie added.

'They got it right,' Jason said.

Another voice chimed in at that point, a female one this time.

'How did it happen, sir?' This was Jenny Stewart, a long-haired brunette, who was one of the more studious pupils in the class. And she loved Shakespeare. Something about the language enthralled her, which Jason considered fair enough. Shakespeare had a definite knack for a phrase. She was never any trouble in class so being questioned like this by her was new.

'I don't know what you've been reading,' Jason said.

'It said on Twitter that you were in a scuffle with a man in a pub and he died as a result.'

'They didn't give the details in the newspapers,' Jason said.

'They do on Twitter,' Allie said.

Jason glanced down at his text of Macbeth. They had been approaching the bloody conclusion. Perhaps Macbeth would escape his demise in this lesson, and one was due for Jason instead. With all eyes fixed on him, Jason had the full attention of his class. If only his discussion of texts was as enthralling.

It did hurt that Jenny Stewart was looking at him in that way. There were pupils in every class that Jason wanted to impress, the serious ones, the ones that excelled in their work, and who he could tell were going to go on to do great things. Jenny had the look of someone who had eyes on far horizons, and she was straightforward in the way she behaved. She was also self-respecting and respectful. Jason liked to be thought of as a good teacher by pupils like Jenny. He wasn't sure how he was going to come across to her now, and others like her in the school.

'But, as word of it has reached your ears, perhaps I ought to explain.'

'Oh do,' Allie said, with a mocking tone.

The curious eyes that Jason found himself looking at in his class mostly echoed that, though there were some pupils, like Jenny, who looked sympathetic and helpful as if willing a reasonable explanation out of him.

'He had been causing my girlfriend problems,' Jason said.

Then he paused. How could he talk about those with his class?

'They had been in a relationship before I knew her, and she'd told him she was finished with him, but he wouldn't accept it.'

Jason was particularly aware of the intensity in the gaze of the girls. He tried hard to think how he could make them understand. Words could open doors. Couldn't he think of even one that might work? Then he did. Stalking, that might do it. They all knew what that word meant.

'He refused to take no for an answer, and he stalked her and terrified her.'

Looking at the faces in front of him, Jason thought he might be heading in the right direction. There was a nodding, and there were looks of understanding; some of his class were rooting for him. Now he had to try to get them all onside.

'When he came into that pub, it was as if he was trying to bring things to a head. He was the one with the agenda. My girlfriend and I were having a quiet drink together. He started talking – reasonably at first. But he became angrier and said he'd had enough. He'd come to reclaim his girlfriend and she was leaving with him. He grabbed her and tried to force her to go with him. I pulled back at him to stop him. He tripped on a stool and fell over, hit his head on a marble tabletop. And that was it.'

There was silence as 4A struggled to take in real adult drama.

'As simple as that,' Jason said. 'As quick as that. He hit his head and that was the end of him. You can imagine how I felt. I was horrified.'

That, of course, was a lie. Jason had been delighted. He'd wanted to jump up and down with joy. But he could hardly say that to his class.

'And then some,' Jenny said. 'I'll bet you were.'

'I would have been pleased,' Allie said. 'Weren't you? You thought he deserved it, didn't you?'

Allie had never shown any understanding of the subtleties of human interaction in the texts they'd been reading together but he'd got straight to the nub of Jason. Oh, yes, Jason had been pleased, which was the problem.

'He did deserve it, sir,' came another voice and Jason hadn't realised teenagers could be so callous.

'It really was an accident, then?' said another.

'What happened with your girlfriend after that?' Jenny wanted to know.

'We've moved on since then,' Jason said, giving an answer he thought would cover it without saying anything.

'But you put yourself on the line for her,' said another girl.

'You rescued her from a stalker,' said another.

'You mean she dropped you after you'd done that for her?' said someone else.

Jason was sure they would have enjoyed hearing all the details of his subsequent failed relationship with Renée had he been willing to share them, not that he would. He was incapable of it. The hurt of how things had ended with Renée was still with him, though Renée hadn't been the one to blame. He was the one who'd left, and, in any case, he knew he was the one at fault for everything that had gone wrong in his life, so he couldn't complain when it all caught up with him.

'And you killed Paul Robertson too?' Allie said.

None of them had dared to directly question him about Paul's murder before but all gloves were off now.

'No,' Jason said.

'But Isla's your girlfriend,' Allie said. 'It stands to reason. You killed that Eddie Caldwell because he was annoying your girl in Edinburgh. And, if you'd do that – which you did – if Paul was treating Isla badly, you could kill him as easily, couldn't you?'

Didn't you? Did someone add that or was that something in Jason's head? He wasn't entirely sure.

He found himself facing thirty pairs of accusing eyes, all apparently convinced he must have killed Paul Robertson as well. For the first time in his teaching career, he felt truly flummoxed.

ELEVEN

At the beginning of Jason and Isla's relationship, she had been the one in need of comfort, but now he was the one on edge and he sought her out for support. He was soon discussing his difficult lesson with 4A. The sympathy in her eyes thrilled.

'But that's unbelievable,' Isla said. 'It's insolence discussing any of that with you.'

'Maybe,' Jason said. 'Or maybe things are a little bit out of the ordinary just now.'

'You should report them.'

'For what? For having anxieties about rumours surrounding their teacher? This is difficult for them to deal with too.'

'That's understanding of you,' Isla said. 'But aren't you being too patient with them?'

'Or not. But I had to try to answer their questions. I probably made a hash of it.'

'Is it true about Eddie Caldwell?'

'Yes, I killed him. Everyone around here knows about it now. No secrets there. I might as well admit it.'

'But they let you walk free.'

'Circumstances. It's difficult to explain. I don't find this easy to talk about.'

'Perhaps you should have discussed it more at the time. That must be why there's that sadness about you. You haven't talked it out. You can't bottle things up. It doesn't work.'

'I suppose you're right,' Jason said.

'What did happen?' she asked.

'My girlfriend at the time was a person called Renée. I thought a lot of her. And I felt for her too. She was a troubled soul. She'd had this awful boyfriend, Eddie Caldwell, the guy I killed later. He was a monster, and no loss to the world, if that makes any difference, but he was still a guy, a young man with his life ahead of him. And I took it from him.'

'So how did you end up killing him?' Isla said.

'I didn't mean to hurt him. We were just pulling and shoving at each other. That's all. He was harassing Renée. I was trying to get him to stop. But I did too good a job of it. He fell over and hit his head on a marble tabletop. One moment he was there, big, nasty, and snarling. The next he was a silent heap on the floor, and no undoing that.

'They ruled it an accidental killing. It was questioned carefully, and I was lucky it was ruled as Involuntary Act Culpable Homicide. If they'd decided it was voluntary, I was in trouble. The thing is he didn't trip over a bar stool. I put my leg in his way to unbalance him, which I had to lie about. That's why he fell over. Was I trying to kill him? I was so pleased about the fact he was dead you might have thought so.'

He had no idea why he had told Isla all of that. He'd never been completely honest with anyone about that incident before. But already he felt the better for it.

Isla gave him a questioning look.

'So, you felt good about it afterwards?'

'Yes. The guy was a creep. Do you know he raped Renée the first time she tried to leave him? He said she belonged to him and didn't have the right to leave.'

'He does sound horrible. So, you were celebrating after his death, huh? Cheering?'

Now Jason gave Isla a questioning look.

'No, of course not.'

Then he paused as he thought some more.

'But I was pleased and shouldn't have been, which I knew. And that made me feel bad. It was as if I'd been given a window into my own soul, and I was surprised by what I found in there.'

Isla held Jason's hand to comfort him. Then her arms were round his and she was whispering in his ear.

'Don't feel so bad about yourself. It was an accident. You couldn't have known that would kill him – and the guy deserved it. I'm proud of you.'

Now she looked Jason in the eyes again.

'You were right to be pleased about what you'd done.'

Despite the sympathy and the fact Isla was holding him close, none of it made him feel any better about himself. He'd enjoyed killing someone and what kind of person did that make him?

* * *

Buchanan wasn't someone Jason wanted to meet up with this often. The inspector had knocked on Jason's door just as Jason had been preparing a meal and he had to switch off the stove and resign himself to cooking his chilli con carne later. Buchanan said he wanted to know if his memory of that night had returned, but it hadn't.

'You said you heard an angry voice. It wasn't directed at you, was it?'

Jason's impression was that there had been a loud discussion between two others, and that was what he told Buchanan. Then he tried to focus on what he definitely did remember, a loud male voice and another sound in reply. Was that a male voice, a female one, or what? Jason cursed Manhattans and cocktails in general. He wasn't going to have one of those again.

'We have a witness who says there was a quarrel and that it was between you and Paul.'

'That didn't happen,' Jason said.

'How do you know?' Buchanan said. 'You don't remember anything. Apparently.'

Jason did not know how to reply to that. If he couldn't recall anything, anything could have happened.

'They've taken long enough to come up with this,' Jason said. 'Why didn't they say this before?'

'We did ask them that,' Buchanan said. 'They said they had a hazy memory of that night too, but their memory has refreshed itself.'

'That doesn't sound reliable.'

'That's what we've yet to decide,' Buchanan said.

'What were we quarrelling about? Or has that not come back to them yet?'

'Isla.'

'Why would I quarrel with Paul about Isla?'

Jason did not like the sound of this; he was being implicated.

'Paul was complaining you'd been pestering Isla. Isla was his wife, and he was warning you off.'

'I hardly knew her. I met her once to talk to before that night.'

'So you claim. But we have a lot of witnesses who swear to a continuing relationship between you and Isla, which makes the scenario of a quarrel between you and Paul convincing. You've fallen for Isla. Paul warns you off. Being drunk you have a physical altercation with him. End of story for Paul. You have killed someone in that fashion before.'

Now Buchanan was beginning to sound like Allie in 4A, and it didn't sound as if he was convinced by Jason's previous verdict. What was the best way to respond to this? Jason settled for belligerence.

'You have a lot of belief in my ability in a fight. More than I have. Not that I even swung at Eddie – as you know. There was a bit of pulling about at each other's arms and he fell over. It was a marble top that did for Eddie not me. It would be a real coincidence if something of the sort happened again.'

'The skull fracture was caused by a blow, in much the same place as Eddie Caldwell suffered his fatal injury. You've experience of the effect of injuries to that area. A swing with a blunt instrument from you? That's possible.'

'I would remember doing something like that.'

Jason desperately attempted to remember more. His mind was still stubbornly blank about that night.

'I want you down at the station for fingerprinting and to have a DNA sample taken.'

'What?'

'The blunt instrument might turn up yet.'

Jason found himself down at Nairn police station, thinking about how the visit would add to his already colourful reputation. He wondered how the police could be this dense – though he should have been asking himself how he could be so stupid.

TWELVE

After that he was seeking out Isla for sympathy again. It seemed to irritate her this time, which Jason was disappointed with when he thought how willing he had been to offer her a shoulder to cry on. But Isla relaxed after a moment, and he found himself looking at her captivating smile again.

'They've been at everybody,' Isla said.

'Paul had a quarrel with someone. That's obvious,' Jason said. 'And there were enough people at that party. One of them must have some idea what happened. Paul's attacker wasn't invisible. Why has no one come forward with the truth?'

'Perhaps they don't want to be involved,' Isla said. 'A lot of people wouldn't want the publicity of a murder investigation.'

'That's the point. It is a murder investigation. Don't they realise how important it is to come forward?'

'Believe me, if Amber thought it would damage her acting career to appear as a witness there's no way she would do it. Neither would Andy. He has a high-profile job in a big legal firm in Aberdeen. Bad publicity wouldn't help him. Lena values her job at Gordonstoun. People can come up with lots of excuses.'

'They can't be that materialistic,' Jason said.

'Try them,' Isla replied. 'If they saw a friend quarrelling with Paul, they might not want to do them the dirty by saying so. They might be shallow but they're not without loyalty.'

'I'm glad they pride themselves on having some virtues,' Jason said. 'One of them said they'd seen me quarrelling with Paul.'

'Did they? Did you?' Isla asked.

Jason stared back at her wondering how to reply, then said, 'No. I didn't quarrel with Paul.' Though there was that half-remembered argument, which he supposed could have been him arguing with Paul.

'A lot of people were in the music room dancing their hearts out,' Isla said, 'once it became too cool to stay outside, though it would have been easy enough not to notice someone slipping out.'

'I'm pleased they had such a good time.'

'Stop worrying about this,' Isla said.

'The police have taken my fingerprints and DNA. I'm not supposed to be feeling anxious?'

'They've taken mine as well – and everybody else's. I don't know why they were slow in getting round to you. Perhaps you were the last person they suspected. They're probably just putting the screw on everybody because they still don't know anything.'

'You're saying they made up that story about me arguing with Paul to put pressure on me? No. They wouldn't invent a witness.'

'How do you know? Maybe they think if they browbeat a person, they'll give themselves up.'

'Did anyone tell you about me and Paul quarrelling that night?'

'No.'

'I wish I could remember what I did – or what anyone else was doing.'

'You mean you really don't remember a thing?'

'Not a lot.'

'How odd.'

Then Isla looked thoughtful for a few moments.

'Could you have killed Paul and not remember it? You do read about people having blackouts when they kill someone and don't remember afterwards that they've done it.'

'I seriously doubt it. I'd be sure to remember something like that. And I've never suffered from a blackout in my life. It was those Manhattans. They sent me to sleep. I wasn't murdering anyone. I was lying flat out snoring.'

Isla looked doubtful which Jason did not like.

'And you don't remember Paul having a swing at me at one point? He was prone to doing that every so often. Always said he regretted it of course.'

'Paul did that?'

'But only now and again.'

'Well, that was good of him.'

Then Isla giggled and that surprised Jason.

'I don't suppose you remember the pink flying elephants either, do you?'

Then there was that schoolgirl titter again, although it was much louder. Jason found himself smirking too. Then a laugh came from him.

'Poor Jason. I could tell you anything happened, and you wouldn't know if it had or not, would you?'

'Maybe,' Jason said. 'But I don't believe in the flying elephants.'

'I should hope not.'

'Did Paul hit you?' he asked her.

Isla paused as she thought of her answer.

'He has done. Oh, don't worry. I made sure he regretted it. I wasn't going to allow it to become a habit.'

'He sounds a horrible man. You were unlucky with him.'

'I loved him, silly.'

'Oh yes. Paul was a wonder.'

Jason supposed he shouldn't say any more about that. And he wished he could remember more about that night.

'You really need someone to look after you, Jason. Don't you? Don't worry. I'm here. I will.'

Jason found himself looking deep into those captivating violet eyes again as Isla switched on her most bewitching smile.

THIRTEEN

Next day, Jason taught his classes and reached the end of them with relief. Then, when he was tidying up his classroom, the father of Allie McPhail turned up. Jason hadn't met Tod before, but he soon introduced himself, and, when Jason thought about it, he did look a bit like an older version of Allie. Jason gave his best version of a professional smile; he hoped it didn't look like the grimace he was feeling. Sometimes, he reflected, when things looked as bad as possible, they just became worse, and he had a strong feeling that was happening.

'What can I do to help?' he asked.

'It's about that discussion you had with Allie's class.'

'Oh, that.'

Jason did his best not to flinch.

'Some parents have concerns,' Tod said.

'The class makes good progress,' Jason said, which it had so far.

'It costs enough to send our children here,' Tod replied, 'and good teaching is the least that's expected. There are other worries.'

'I don't know what they could be,' Jason said. He realised with agony that he was going to have to attempt a stand here. 'But, if you share them, we can discuss them.'

'It's a matter of public record that you killed someone in the past. Did you disclose that when you applied for a position in this school? You must have been asked to disclose something like that.'

'It was Involuntary Culpable Homicide, which doesn't have to be declared when applying for jobs,' Jason said, 'but I did. The school knew all about it.'

'Did they?'

'Yes. Look, maybe I could explain it to you. An accident occurred, which is how it's described in the public record. I was defending my girlfriend. I didn't start the argument and there were witnesses to that. The guy happened to hit his head against a marble tabletop in a scuffle. I couldn't have foreseen that happening.'

'You got away with murder once, but it's happened again.'

That remark stung. Jason's attempt to appease had certainly not worked. He would have to make his defence as stout as he could.

'There's such a thing as slander,' he said, 'and this is a public place.'

'With no witnesses,' Tod said, looking around him.

'Perhaps there should be,' Jason said. 'Perhaps we should be continuing this conversation in front of my head of department.'

'That you're under investigation by the police for the murder of Paul Robertson is fact, not slander.'

'Look, it wasn't my fault,' Jason said. 'I don't know anything about it.'

'And you attended a drugs party. There's such a thing as moral turpitude, Mr Sutherland.'

'What?' Jason said.

'At this school, teachers can be dismissed for that reason.'

Yes, Jason had wondered at that phrase in his contract, and wondered how those words could be defined. Did it mean he could be dismissed without having done anything?

'It is of obvious concern to parents that the person in charge of teaching their children might be a murderer. Teachers are moral guardians. They are role models. They can't behave in the way you have. I'll be calling a meeting of the Parents' Association and steps will be taken, Mr Sutherland. I can assure you of that.'

Jason believed him. He had heard of Mr McPhail, Chairman of the Parents' Association, and had been warned not to cross him. McPhail was a man very sure of his own opinions. He was also a well-off businessman who owned a potato wholesale firm. Whether he understood much of anything apart from potatoes, Jason didn't know, but Mr McPhail was used to being master of what he surveyed.

He wondered what Tod had been like in class. He would have been large, boorish, and used to bullying to get things his own way, much like Allie. Jason thought that if he'd given Allie higher marks that might have helped him in this situation, but it was too late now.

To Jason's relief, Tod McPhail turned and left. The self-righteous expression on Tod's face had terrified him. Tod was a man with a mission, not that Jason understood how he could be so judgemental. Jason had not killed Paul Robertson, and he wasn't even in custody for it, so Tod McPhail shouldn't be so sure that he had. Then again, Jason knew he had killed someone – Eddie Caldwell – which he himself would never be able to forget. Perhaps judgement was catching up on him. Had he thought he could escape it forever?

* * *

Two days later Jason was teaching a class as normal and hoping his problems were blowing over, when he found himself being directed towards the headmaster's office, where he met a strangely calm Dougie Lawson. It was unusual to be taken out of a class for an interview with him and Jason felt anything but tranquil.

'I'm sorry, Jason,' was the first thing Lawson said, which was ominous. In Jason's experience, when a headmaster said he was sorry, he wasn't, but the person he was addressing would be.

'This is an independent school,' he continued, 'and you need to be careful about your relationship with parents. I understand you had a meeting with Mr McPhail.'

'Yes?' Jason said.

He thought McPhail had moved fast if he'd been round other parents already.

'The Parents' Association had an emergency meeting last night,' Lawson said.

He had been quick. Very.

'They don't want you teaching classes in this school again.'

Summary judgement, Jason thought.

'I tried to defend you. I said your behaviour as a teacher has been exemplary since you arrived. They said how disappointed they were you had ever been appointed. This has got me into trouble, Jason.'

'I see.'

'So, I have to extricate myself, which I won't do by going against parents.'

Parental power. Dougie had warned Jason about that when he first arrived.

'Obviously, I explained that I did know about your past. As I admitted to them, it was obviously questioned whether you should be appointed because of that, but your teaching record was exemplary, and you have a fine degree. And you were vindicated in court – as far as possible.'

'I see,' Jason said.

It felt odd that Jason could find no more to say when his feelings were boiling up inside him in the way they were.

'Parents say they should have been consulted before your appointment was made. Not that there is usually any need for a head to consult with parents before making appointments. The process would take forever if we always did that. But they repeated that I should have done before you were offered a job here, which is all very well in hindsight. Nobody could have foreseen what was going to happen at Mark Landy's pool that night – as I told them – but they didn't listen. They're concerned. They say they don't want anyone involved with drugs teaching their children. I did tell them you'd said you didn't know there would be drugs at that party, the problem being that, in the court of public opinion, nobody believes that.'

'I've never taken drugs in my life.'

'And not everyone can say that,' Lawson said. 'These same parents may very well have experimented with something when they were younger, which is neither here nor there. You're the one in the dock. Not that it's their only concern.'

'They're overreacting,' Jason said. 'Surely they can be persuaded to see that.'

'They also say you've been having an affair with a married woman.'

'Not true, and even if it was, so what?'

As soon as the words came out of Jason's mouth, he wondered if he should have said that.

'On top of that business of attending a sex and drugs party.'

'Who said anything about a sex party?'

'I'm sure you're right, but rumour has taken wings, and you can't deny you're being investigated for murder. In parents' eyes, you're a wrong'un, and nothing I could say in your defence convinced them otherwise. They don't want you teaching another class here, and, if I value my job, I daren't let you.'

'What?'

'You are suspended.'

'What does that mean?'

'On full pay, and you will receive a letter telling you of the date of your hearing. Present will be me, my assistant head, and the head of the Board, another one of our parents. You will be allowed a union representative.'

'What?'

'But the end result will be that you'll be dismissed. They don't care if you go to an industrial tribunal or not. They're just gunning for you.'

'But—' Jason said.

'Do close the door on your way out.'

FOURTEEN

Feeling in desperate need of emotional support now, Jason sent an urgent text to Isla, who told him to come round. She met him at the door and led him into the lounge.

If he'd been in a better mood, he could have appreciated the room more, but even so he couldn't help noticing again that view over waves stretching out. And on the other side of the firth lay rolling hills. How could anything be awry in such a space? But it was.

Jason seated himself on a chair that would normally have been the epitome of comfort but which, in the mood he was in, wasn't. The Jackson Pollock still hung on the main white wall and Jason studied that. With the money Mark Landy earned, Jason assumed it was genuine. It was a vibrant kaleidoscope of yellow and black that made up an abstract pattern that reflected the chaos Jason was feeling inside himself. He looked away from it again.

'Bloody school,' Isla was saying. 'That was unfair of them – suspending you. Do they have the legal right to do that?'

'According to my contract, which gives them considerable leeway with that sort of thing. There's a bit in it about moral turpitude, though it doesn't define what that is.'

'A handy vague term to use when dismissing someone you don't like,' Isla said.

'And they're feeling more than dislike,' Jason said.

'I don't suppose they've made any effort to look at it from your point of view.'

'I don't think so.'

For once, Isla seemed at a loss for words. Then she laughed and Jason wondered how she could manage to do that.

'You not only murder people but you go to sex parties, and you take drugs.'

Then she laughed again.

'And what's funny about that?' Jason said.

'There is a ludicrous side to it.'

'I wish you would explain it to me.'

'Jason, that's what I love about you. You're such an innocent. You? Guilty of any of that? No one in their right mind would think that of you. And here you are, suspended for all of it.'

Then she giggled and couldn't stop herself. Oh no, Jason thought. Not another of her adolescent moods.

'It's all very well,' Jason said. 'I haven't a rich daddy to fall back on.'

'Right enough. I'm surprised my father allows someone from your background to set foot in the house.'

And another giggle erupted.

'You're not aristocracy,' Jason said.

'Film aristocracy maybe,' Isla said, then gave yet another giggle. 'But I am sorry, I ought to be taking this seriously. I would too if it wasn't so silly. Your school's taken leave of its senses.'

'I agree about the irrationality of the school governors, but I don't see anything light-hearted about this.'

'No,' Isla said. 'You don't. That's the problem. Though I must admit I probably wouldn't in your shoes. Let me fetch you a Manhattan. Nothing ever seems so bad when you've had your first Manhattan of the evening.'

'I definitely don't want one of those.'

'Poor Jason. The world's against you.'

'And then some.'

'I suppose the mention of cocktails does bring back bad memories. I'll make it a gin and tonic.'

She disappeared, then returned with matching drinks. She put Jason's on the table beside him, but Jason didn't touch it.

Sipping her own gin relaxed Isla at least. Jason had wondered at the suggestion of hysteria somewhere in her deliberately light-hearted tone. Was there an inability to cope with the seriousness of the situation? But now the note in her voice changed.

'We have to talk about this, Jason,' she said. 'Bad things just seem to happen to you. First Eddie Caldwell, now this.'

'I've been trying to talk about it,' Jason replied.

He'd reached the end of his patience but managed to bite back a more cutting remark. He reached for the gin and tonic and sipped; in the silence that ensued he gave further thought to things.

'I've never stopped feeling guilty about Eddie Caldwell,' he said. 'I feel as if I got away with something there. I know it was an accident. How could I know he would hit his head on a marble tabletop and kill himself? But I was pleased he was dead. That was the end of Renée's problems. There was no coming back from that for Eddie.

And I knew it was wrong to be glad about that. It made me a murderer at heart if not by intention. But that didn't stop me being pleased I'd done that, and still doesn't. Is there something wrong with me?'

'What do you mean?'

'I don't know.' Jason sipped gin and thought a bit more. 'But that changed me. It's as if… I've separated off somewhere else. I'm in a different place from other people. They live their lives in the way they should. They feel things in the way they should. They laugh and enjoy life. I'm trapped somewhere else. My emotions are frozen somehow. I don't feel for other people in the way I should.'

'You don't?'

He noticed the thoughtful expression on Isla's face as she watched him. Perhaps she could work this out for him.

'I feel for you though,' he said.

'You do?'

He looked at her and the violet eyes and the smile opened towards him.

'I don't know,' he said. 'It's as if the only time I do feel anything is when I'm with you.'

'Well, that sounds hopeful – I think.'

But Isla's giggle was nervous.

'I'd been…' Jason searched for words. 'It's as if I feel low – all the time. And it gives me a prism that I see life through. Everything is sort of dark and I don't see hope in situations in the way I used to.'

'That sounds awful,' Isla said.

'It was killing Eddie that did it to me. I couldn't stand living in Edinburgh after that. It was as if I could see him everywhere, lying on that pub floor. I needed to get away from that image burning my mind.'

'I'm sure you did,' Isla said.

'Coming here was a fresh start. Though I don't know. I don't seem to have left anything behind. I can still see him now. I think I always will.'

'You need to find a way of moving on.'

'I don't think I can. That's the problem.'

'Surely not?' Isla said. 'You'll heal in time, Jason. Don't worry about it. Look, Jason, if you didn't mean to kill him you didn't. You're being oversensitive.'

'I've tried telling myself that,' Jason said. 'It doesn't work. I don't know why. And now this has happened. Another person has died, and I've got involved in that somehow and I've lost my job. I don't handle things well, do I?'

'Have you talked with your union rep about your suspension?' Isla asked.

'I've a meeting arranged for tomorrow night.'

'At least then you'll have more idea about what your actual rights are. Tell me more about this Tod McPhail. Where did he sound as if he was coming from?'

'From the place of an arrogant prick.'

'Now, Jason.'

'You should have heard him.'

'Was he that bad?'

'It had to be the father of the worst pupil I teach. His son, Allie, is a loudmouth, lazy braggart who bullies everybody in sight – and it's as if his father is acting as his mouthpiece.'

'The relationship they make with the teacher is the same as the one they have with their parents. That's how it was explained to me,' Isla said. 'They rebel at home and get in trouble for it, then take it out on the teacher.'

'Maybe,' Jason said. 'I don't know. It was me his father was going on about, a moral degenerate unfit to teach his son, or any class in that school. He probably thinks I'm a drug dealer as well. I've never met a reaction like that. Couldn't he try to deal with situations rationally instead of trusting rumours so much?'

'He's an idiot. You're right.'

Isla looked thoughtful.

'He's being used by his son,' she said. 'Allie can't succeed in causing trouble in your class, so he gets his father to do it.'

'Yes,' Jason said. 'That probably sums it up.'

'The whole thing's seriously stupid,' Isla said, but she didn't look as if she was listening anymore. She seemed lost in thought.

Then Mark Landy walked in.

'Hi, Jason,' he said.

He held out his hand and gave his huge grin. Jason held out his hand in return and did his best to manage an approximation of a smile.

'It's serious in here,' Mark said. 'Is everything OK?'

'Jason's being sacked from his job,' Isla said.

'Sorry to hear it,' Mark said.

He gave Jason an expression of sympathy that was almost exaggerated though it looked genuine enough. Jason wondered how anyone could manage to smile so often.

'Our pool party,' Isla said.

'What about it?' Mark asked.

'You didn't know about the dope?' Jason said.

'Was there dope there?'

'Only some coke,' Isla said.

'Only?' Jason said.

'You didn't tell me about that,' Mark said to Isla.

But he didn't look surprised to Jason.

'You definitely shouldn't be doing coke,' Mark said. 'Have you done it before?'

'Dad,' Isla said, not gracing this with an answer.

It was obvious to Jason that Mark had known all about the coke, which meant he must have turned a blind eye. It had been out of sight, out of mind to him. Then, as if reading Jason's mind, Mark replied to that.

'Young people being who they are, I'd have been surprised there was never the occasional something going on, but I didn't expect anything like the comeback there's been from that party, and I certainly wouldn't expect anyone to be murdered. And it was Paul. I mean. How could anything like that happen? Believe me, we're giving the police our full co-operation to catch the bastard.'

Then he gave Jason an appraising look. He didn't think Jason might have done it, did he?

'But what on earth reason are they giving for dismissing you?' he asked.

'Rumour and gossip,' Isla said.

'So, there's been talk amongst parents. They can't dismiss you because of that, can they?'

'They're sure they can,' Jason said.

'It sounds dodgy to me,' Mark said.

'Moral turpitude. That's what they're claiming,' Jason said.

'They have to establish it though,' Mark said, 'which they can't without anything more than gossip.'

Jason sighed. Mark had made things sound more hopeful, but Jason doubted if they were.

'What you need is a good lawyer,' Mark said.

'I doubt if I could afford it,' Jason said.

'Still, you ought to get one,' Mark said.

Jason tried to give thought to that, but he was in so much despair he didn't think anything would do any good anyway.

FIFTEEN

At Andy's invitation, Isla, Ellie, Joanne, Lena, Amber, Andy, and Jason, the people who'd been at Isla's fateful pool party, had now met up at The Bandstand.

Isla had the look of an anxiety basket case who couldn't stop chewing her nails, and Ellie resembled a bewildered rabbit. There had been a deterioration in them all, Jason supposed, though there was also some pretence at composure. Joanne's detached expression might have suggested she'd rather be writing her novel. Amber's acting skills were at the fore with a masterly inscrutable expression. Lena's usual vacant-doll act was more convincing than ever as she really didn't know what was going on, which put her in the same boat as everyone else. Andy, the puppet-master responsible for everyone's attendance, looked slightly surprised they were all there, if smug about it. Jason was emotionally overdrawn after everything that had been going on and supposed that was exactly how he looked.

Andy ordered drinks and it was surprising how many orange squashes and ginger beers were on order. Jason thought they must be feeling they needed all their senses about them though Isla had ordered an early evening gin and Andy had a healthy double of Macallan in front of him. Jason had a spring water sitting there and felt like pouring it over his own head to make himself properly alert.

And there they were, seated at a table in a corner in The Bandstand, eyes firmly on each other.

'We need to discuss what happened at the pool party,' Andy was saying.

'Should we be doing that?'

Lena was pointing an elegantly manicured pink nail at Andy, though she looked fraught rather than alluring.

'Why not?' Andy said.

'We're not supposed to collude about statements,' Isla said.

'We've already given those,' Andy replied.

'So, what are we discussing?' Isla asked.

'What happened,' Andy said. 'We all need to come to terms with it. And I'd like to try to work out what occurred that night.'

'We should leave it to the police,' Amber said.

'I'm not suggesting a Sherlock Holmes bit of sleuthing,' Andy said.

'So, what are you proposing?' Amber said.

'They seem to think I had a massive argument with Paul. Where did that come from?'

A sea of inquiring faces looked back at him as if to suggest no one had any idea.

'Out of thin air, huh?' Andy said. 'That's not likely. That suggestion came from one of you. Which one of you was it?'

'They seemed to think I had one too,' Jason said.

Everyone gave each other questioning looks.

'Have you considered it might be something the police were making up to help them question people?' Isla said.

That suggestion from Isla again. Jason wondered if it was likely.

'The police can't do that,' Lena said.

'You're telling me that was an interrogation technique?' Andy said.

As no one had anything to say in reply, Andy took a sip of his Macallan while he mulled this over.

'Did anyone hear any arguments at all?'

No one said anything.

'Remarkable,' Andy said. 'And nobody saw anything suspicious that might have led up to Paul's death?'

Jason found himself chasing vague memories of raised voices that did nothing but fade further away.

'Isla, as he was your husband, I assume he was with you most of the time.'

'No,' Isla said. 'I spent some time with Jason, then with Lena and Joanne.'

'You weren't with Lena all night,' Andy said.

'I didn't say all night.'

'Not even much of it.'

Andy turned to Lena.

'You pulled the band leader, didn't you?' he said to her. 'And disappeared into an upstairs bedroom. I assume that's where you went. I didn't exactly follow you.'

Lena's face now held an embarrassed expression which Andy took to mean yes.

Ah, Jason thought, that's where the rumours of the sex party could have come from.

'Do we know where Joanne was all evening?' Isla asked suddenly.

'What do you mean?' Andy said.

'Oh, yes,' Joanne said. 'Let's all ask about Joanne. Why not? Why are you asking about me?'

She looked insulted.

'I know about you and Paul,' Isla said. 'Was he finishing with you? Did you have an argument about that?'

'What?'

Joanne looked dumbfounded. It felt odd to see her at a loss. Then she recovered herself.

'An affair with Paul? Wasn't everybody having one of those?'

That took Isla aback. She looked as if she wanted to spit at Joanne.

'I say,' Amber said, 'hold back a bit, won't you, Joanne?'

'So,' Isla said, 'after Paul finished with you and you murdered him, how did you spend the rest of the evening, Joanne?'

'Let's all relax, shall we?' Andy said.

'Are you saying you saw Joanne kill Paul?' Ellie said to Isla.

'No,' she replied.

'But you saw them arguing together?' Andy said.

Isla didn't say anything at first.

Then she said, 'I'll bet they did.'

'You should watch what you're saying,' Joanne said. 'There are a lot of accusations coming out of you, and you haven't got proof of anything.'

'That doesn't mean it's not true.'

The two women contented themselves with glaring at each other for the moment though Jason thought either of them could easily start pummelling away at the other.

Then Joanne said, 'What if I did have an affair with him? He was available. You should have looked after him better.'

Isla looked close to losing it at that point. Then she did, her face snarling as she got to her feet to launch herself at Joanne. But Andy held her back.

'Temper, temper, Isla.'

'She's a bitch,' Isla said. 'She needs her eyes scratching out.'

It was a good thing Andy had such strong arms. Then as suddenly as Isla's fury had erupted, it seemed to go, and she sat down again, though her look towards Joanne was still full of hate.

Andy put on an authoritative voice as he said, 'We might get somewhere discussing this if we can all keep calm. Does everybody remember exactly what they did all evening? That's what we need to concentrate on, writing down a timeline of the things we know that happened, not things we're speculating about.'

Everybody was still looking at Isla in alarm and were relieved to be given the distraction of thinking of something else.

'We were all squiffy,' Amber said, 'but I remember everything all right.'

'After it became too cool outside, most of us went into the music room – with the band – to dance,' Ellie said.

'That's where I spent most of my time,' Joanne said with a pointed expression, 'as everyone else who was there can verify.'

'So, we were together at the beginning,' Andy said, 'and then some of us separated into different places.'

'Yes,' they replied.

'Which is when anybody could have dispatched Paul and put him in the pool without being seen,' Andy said.

A group of assenting faces looked back at him.

'But it wasn't any of us,' Ellie said.

'OK,' Andy said. From a briefcase – which Jason hadn't noticed before – Andy produced paper and pens. Then he said OK again, as if attempting to mesmerise everyone into agreement.

'I want you all to write down who you talked to and where you were from the beginning of the night till the end.'

'We've done that for the police,' Jason said.

'And they're not going to share their investigations with us, are they?' Andy said.

'I suppose not,' Jason said. 'But what are you going to do with all this?'

'Share it with everybody,' Andy said. 'And we can put our heads together and try to work out what happened.'

'Shouldn't we be leaving that to the police?' Isla said.

Nobody looked as if they wanted to disagree with that. Except Joanne.

'Odd you should be the one saying that?' Joanne said.

'Really?' Isla said.

'The first suspect is the spouse,' Joanne continued.

'What would you know about it?' Isla said.

She looked as if she might erupt again, which is when Andy spoke once more.

'Normally, it is,' Andy said, 'though I'm sure that's not what happened this time.'

'See. I'm being agreed with by a lawyer,' Joanne said.

'Who doesn't work in criminal law,' Isla added, she didn't look any calmer.

'But he's right,' Joanne said.

Isla pulled a face at her.

'You're saying I did it?' she said. 'I should never have agreed to come here.'

'It's a pity you did,' Joanne said. 'And it's much more likely to have been you than me. I think you did it.'

'Really?' Isla said. 'We'll find out, won't we?'

She got up again but to everybody's relief simply picked up her jacket ready to leave.

'Don't go,' Andy said. 'I shouldn't have said that, and Joanne shouldn't. I'm sorry, Isla. Look, if we all write things down, we might have a better idea how to protect ourselves when the police question us again. They put a real squeeze on me at one point, and they've been having a go at you, Jason, haven't they?'

Jason nodded his head. Isla didn't look convinced or any calmer but sat down again. People looked warily at each other, then Lena nodded, and others did too.

'It'll help you protect yourself too, Isla,' Andy said.

As Isla gave thought to this, some of the truculence left her face and she reached her hand out towards the paper and pens – as did everyone else. They were passed around, and some people disagreed with what certain others had written down, and corrections were made. Slowly, a timeline for the evening was agreed on. At least they would all be telling the same story to the police now. But it had taken them no nearer to finding out who had killed Paul. Had it been one of them? According to the timeline they now had, no. Might it have been one of the band, even if none of them knew any of the others personally?

After that, they started to relax a bit more, even Isla, though there was still a sulk on her face. The business of the evening was over. It might protect them a bit better, which was at least one result of the evening, but the dilemma remained. A murder had happened. They had all been there and none of them had seen anything – or admitted they had – but someone had still killed Paul. They chatted and tried to behave more normally but a feeling of lassitude now overcome them. There was nothing in these timelines to show who the murderer was, and the evening felt as if it had been a waste of time. After his energetic beginning, even Andy had given up on discussing the events of that night, and people started to drift off.

Andy wasn't prepared to let go of Jason that easily. He wanted to talk to him about his interviews with the police. What exactly had they wanted to know from him? That was how Andy became Jason's alibi for what happened next.

SIXTEEN

The news broadcast Jason watched on his TV next morning was another dramatic one. There had been a second murder in Nairn. Oh no, Jason thought. What was going on?

A man had been found dead in his back garden, sprawled out, a gaping wound in his skull, blood everywhere. At one point in the evening, he had gone out to check on sounds he had heard and hadn't come back in. The victim was named as Tod McPhail.

Jason felt like jumping up and down with delight when he heard that and wondered at his lack of sensitivity. He supposed this was his callous streak again, the one he'd become so aware of on the night of Eddie Caldwell's death. Something in him wondered how he could be expected to feel otherwise. Tod had caused Jason a lot of trouble; he'd led the campaign to have him sacked.

Jason wondered if this would rescue him from his situation at work but didn't think so. Once parents had a teacher in their sights, they wouldn't let him go. At least revenge had felt sweet, even if he had no hand in it.

Then Jason began to calm down, as his mind worked through everything. His worst enemy might be dead but how could it have happened and who could have done it?

Jason's first reaction was that he wouldn't put it past Allie, but there was a huge difference between classroom misdemeanours and murder. Allie was a boorish teenager and that was all. There was no reason to suppose him capable of anything like this. So, who was?

Jason was starting to feel a chill in his bones. Paul had been murdered – and now this. He assumed the same person had done both murders, which meant this was a dangerous situation. Who might be next? He could only hope the killer would stop now but what kind of rationale did they have for what they were doing and would they?

God, this was serious. What was going on? Jason felt even more out of his depth than he had after Paul's death. He had been trying to escape when he came up here but perhaps he ought to flee Nairn now.

Tod was dead. Jason thought of his florid face. It had been ugly but so full of life with all that self-righteous vindication. Tod had been an energetic man who ran his own business, and had been filled with the self-importance of that, and now it was drained from him. Jason pictured his body flat out in his own back garden, motionless, blood gushing. He had been cut down to the size everyone is in the end, but it had happened before his time. Was Jason starting to feel sympathy for him? Perhaps he was redeemable after all. Perhaps.

Then the doorbell rang and there was a policeman standing outside Jason's door again. Jason wondered what alibi he could come up with because he could not deny having a motive for this murder.

'We would like you to come down to the police station,' the constable said. Not words Jason wanted to hear.

He soon found himself seated opposite a serious-faced Buchanan, wondering how he could get out of this one.

'I'm told you've been suspended from school,' was the first thing Buchanan said to which Jason replied yes as there was nothing else to say.

'What are your feelings about that?'

'I don't like it,' Jason replied, but did not elaborate.

He supposed he should have some strategy for surviving this interview, but he didn't. His short answers had probably come across as surly, but did that make him look guilty or innocent – or just fed up? Buchanan drummed his fingers as he looked at Jason thoughtfully.

'It isn't a criminal offence to be suspended from my job,' Jason said. 'You can't have brought me down here to ask me about that.'

Jason had discovered his strategy, a mixture of confusion and aggression, if it was a tactic as such. It was just how he felt.

'Some people would think it was unfair,' Buchanan said. 'You hadn't misbehaved at school, and yet there you were, stuck at home, waiting to hear the next decision about your teaching career.'

'We've established that I didn't like it.'

'Parents were the moving force behind that suspension,' Buchanan said.

'They pay for their children's education which means they're entitled to express opinions.'

'But you must have thought they'd been unjust.'

'You're putting words in my mouth.'

'But you must have done.'

'As I said, I didn't like it.'

'Tod McPhail was the one leading the parents on this issue, which you knew. You had a meeting with him when he must have expressed his feelings. What reply did you make?'

'I didn't have a rowdy argument with him. He's a parent – or was…' Jason's words faded away.

'Which doesn't answer my question.'

'I just tried to explain my position. That was all I could do. I didn't murder Paul Robertson and I didn't know there were going to be drugs at that party. I told him I was innocent.'

'And now he's dead.'

'Which I had nothing to do with.'

'How did it happen, Mr Sutherland?'

'I don't know. I wasn't there.'

Buchanan gave Jason a particularly icy stare.

'For an innocent person, you have a bad habit of finding yourself in compromising situations.'

Jason was ruffled by this, and his voice began to rise.

'Perhaps they find me. It's not as if I go looking for them.'

Buchanan's look became fiercer.

'You're a person of extreme interest in this case.'

Jason's voice became louder. 'I am? I can't say I find that interesting at all.'

Jason wondered if sarcasm was wise and thought not. This was a policeman. Shouting wouldn't be sensible either, even though Jason knew his frustration was rising. Despite knowing buttoning his lip was a good idea, he continued to make replies.

'You're wasting your time with me.'

He had meant to say something placatory, but that wasn't.

'I don't know anything about Mr McPhail's death,' he added, defiance still in his voice.

He wished he could find something to say that might help himself.

'It was a tragedy and I feel for his son – whom I teach – and the rest of his family. Whoever did it must be some sort of madman.'

That all had to be said, even though Jason was still glad the bastard was dead, and he had no sympathy for Tod

McPhail's spoiled, selfish son. He just had to hope none of that showed.

'You have a motive for this murder,' Buchanan said.

'You've established I have a motive for resenting him. That's not the same thing. I'd no reason to kill him. What would be the sense in that? It would lead to the police turning up at my door, which is what has happened. I'm not stupid. I wouldn't deliberately put myself in that situation.'

'Murder never makes sense, Mr Sutherland, except to the murderer. And you do have motive for this.'

Buchanan was like a dog chasing a scent; nothing would stop him.

'All I can say is I didn't do it.'

'Thank you.'

Jason wondered what that meant. Buchanan was looking deliberately at him again, and Jason wished he would stop doing that.

'We've established your position. Now we need to know your alibi. Where were you between the hours of seven and nine yesterday evening?'

'At least I've got one,' Jason said.

'Which is?'

'I was at The Bandstand with the others who were at that pool party.'

'Why were you meeting up with them?'

'We know each other. You've established that before.'

'Mockery doesn't help, Mr Sutherland.'

Had that been his tone? He should stop being so angry. He wished he could manage it.

'We met up at The Bandstand at about half past six, but most people had left by half seven. I stayed on with Andy McAulay – for a couple of hours.'

'Andy McAulay?'

Jason's alibi seemed only to have deepened Buchanan's suspicions though Jason wasn't sure why.

Buchanan continued with his questions, and Jason with his evasions, until the end of the painful interview. Jason wasn't sure what, if anything, Buchanan had established by the end of it, but at least he allowed Jason to leave, which meant he couldn't have enough to arrest him.

SEVENTEEN

As Jason had become almost an accepted part of the family, it had become natural for him to turn up at Isla's home to see her, and Mark welcomed him with an affable smile. This time he wanted to talk to Jason before fetching Isla.

He poured coffee, and Jason leaned back in a chair and sipped. He had warmed to Mark. Jason had never known a celebrity before and was flattered by the attention Mark was giving him. He might have expected there to be something condescending in the manner of a famous film star, but Mark had an easy charm.

'I still can't get over how good you've been for Isla,' Mark said. 'And I can see why she's fond of you.'

'Thanks,' Jason said, thinking she was the one who'd been good for him.

'I've always had to look out for her.'

'Have you?'

'She's always been a fragile flower, our Isla.'

Jason hadn't thought of Isla as fragile; she seemed tough to him, even if he had seen how hurt she could be.

'I could never understand why she had such difficulty settling into schools,' Mark went on. 'She moved about a bit when she was secondary age. There are so many problem teachers, aren't there? And too many bullying pupils. She was expelled from one school, which was most unjust. Another girl started the fight with her, and, of course, Isla defended herself, then was given the blame for attacking the other girl, which was bunkum.'

Jason hadn't known about any of that. That must have been hard for Isla to cope with.

'And I always had to be extra-protective of her because her mother died when she was eleven.'

Jason had known about that as Isla had told him.

Mark continued. 'It was a road accident and Isla was in the car as well. Ellen lost control when she was going round a corner. There was ice on the road and Ellen went into a skid and couldn't recover from it. She smashed into a tree.'

'Isla's had difficult times in her life,' Jason said.

'And she's having a difficult time of it again. She's lost Paul.'

'Are the police no nearer to finding out who did that?' Jason asked.

'No. They've been at you again, you said?'

'About this parent at school who died. They seem to think I have a motive.'

'They do?'

'Not that I would do anything like that,' Jason said

'Of course not,' Mark said, but a bit too quickly, Jason thought. 'Everybody being so suspicious about you for Paul's death was awful. The way people's minds work. I'm sorry that being a friend for Isla has caused you problems.'

That sounded good but Jason did notice the curious look Mark was giving him.

'But you didn't kill this Tod McPhail, did you?'

Jason gulped. He hadn't been expecting that question.

'Definitely not,' he said.

Mark now had a most understanding and confidential look on his face.

'Because I could understand it if you did.'

Jason didn't reply immediately. He became conscious of the clock ticking and the caw of a seagull somewhere outside. Jason was wondering what Mark thought he was talking about.

'It was murder,' Jason said. 'How could anyone be understanding about that? And I didn't do it.'

'That's what you have to say, and I applaud you for it. Quite right.'

Mark Landy was annoying Jason now. Jason was beginning to wonder if he'd ever really seen this famous actor. Behind the genuine and caring attitude Mark had always shown, perhaps he had never been there at all. Because despite the genial and understanding expression Mark held in his face now, there was this menace in him. Then Mark laughed, the brown eyes softened, and he flashed his most effusive smile.

'Sorry, Jason. Had to test you there. You don't mind, do you?'

He gave another broad smile, then laughed again.

'You're so right, Jason. Never admit to it.'

And he gave another laugh.

And Jason did not understand why Mark would find any of this funny. Perhaps he didn't get the humour of the entertainment world. Then Mark put a serious look on his face.

'I have heard all about that bastard Eddie Caldwell. Did you know he beat his wife?'

Jason was surprised to find out that from Mark. Hitting his wife was something Jason might have expected Eddie to do, but it was news to him that he had.

Mark went on. 'The relationship he had before Renée did not end well. She divorced him.'

'I knew that,' Jason said.

'I had enquiries made. So that I could help, Jason. That's why. He was charged for assaulting her once. But she withdrew her evidence.'

'So, what is it you're telling me?' Jason asked.

'I wouldn't waste any sleep over killing him.'

'It was an accident,' Jason said.

'Of course it was,' Mark said. 'Not that it matters much if it wasn't. That's all I'm saying.'

'You mean you think I murdered him as well?'

'Of course not.'

'Where are you going with this, Mark? For once and for all, I did not kill Tod McPhail.'

'Was that what I said? What I meant was' – there was hesitation on Mark's face – 'I get it. In your position, there are arguments you need to make.'

And Jason didn't like the sound of that.

'Whether you did the crime or not, they're the same arguments.'

'My position?'

What was he saying?

'You know you're a suspect? The police have been questioning you.'

'I have an alibi. I was nowhere near.'

'Who's your alibi?'

'Andy.'

'Ah.'

Mark pondered this, then seemed to deem himself satisfied.

'Maybe you'll be OK.'

'I'd better be,' Jason said.

'But if the police do come back, here's the number of my lawyer. Don't bother about the expense.'

He gave Jason a card which Jason looked at with stupefaction before putting it in his wallet. He was still hoping there would be no need of a solicitor.

Then Isla appeared, and took the conversation somewhere else, but some of Jason's thoughts remained on that talk with Mark. Did Mark think he was a double murderer? Just as bad, did he condone it? What kind of person was Mark Landy?

EIGHTEEN

Jason couldn't believe it when Renée turned up. All those months when she had only existed as someone at the other end of an occasional email, and there she was in person outside his door. He ushered her in.

He wasn't sure what his feelings were about this. He was glad to see her. That was the easy bit, but other emotions swirled around.

He found himself staring again as he tried to take her in. Renée didn't have film star looks, which, when he thought about it now, was in her favour. Her face was a bit square for that, her build a bit broad, but she did have such a lovely healthy prettiness.

And she presented herself so well. Her unobtrusive make-up was carefully applied, her scent delicate but clear, and he knew her dyed blonde bob cut was only allowed to show dark roots on occasion. There was a freshness about her that lit up Jason's flat straight away.

There was a smile on her face, but one that was nothing like those of the Landys. It was natural, not one that said look at me and see how genuine I am.

'It's good to see you,' Jason said, which it was.

He was also wondering what she was doing there but did not start off by saying that. He didn't want to offend her; he had missed her. Yes, he realised, that was the other feeling there. And guilt at leaving her behind.

She stood in the middle of Jason's cramped, rented flat and surveyed it. Only after giving the place a good, long look did she sit down on a seat, which swallowed her up, as Jason's chairs tended to do. This he had always found a bit worrying. The padding on the upholstery was overdone, and he often wondered about the sturdiness of the frames. He didn't think it a good idea to sit down hard on his seats.

'So, this is where you've escaped to,' she said.

The look in her eye was challenging.

Jason looked round the room too, not liking the way it must appear to Renée. It had never struck him before how tawdry his furnishings were. Every expense had been spared. And there was such a temporary feeling to the place, as if it was somewhere anyone only stayed in for so long.

'You have to live somewhere,' Jason said.

'But not Edinburgh?' she replied.

'No.'

He did not elaborate.

'I've missed you,' she said.

'It's complicated,' Jason replied, 'but I've missed you too.'

It was true. Renée had been the love of his life. He felt no remorse about defending her against Eddie Caldwell so he shouldn't have needed to walk away from everything. The problem after the trial was that the emotions had been too strong to cope with. Despite the lack of regret, or perhaps because of it, there had been feelings of guilt, and they'd weighed on him. He'd sat around for a long time in a brain fog, unable to function. His feelings had been so overwhelming he couldn't concentrate on a simple television programme for images in his mind of Eddie falling and hitting his head off that table. He'd needed to run away as far as he could, and then even further. He should have been able to explain that to Renée, but he hadn't.

'You shouldn't have walked out and left,' she said.

They stared at each other for a moment. He was the one who looked away.

'I said why I needed to do that,' Jason said. He had mumbled various excuses at the time, though none of them explained it. 'And I don't…'

'Don't what?' she said as he let the sentence hang unfinished.

'I couldn't cope with things in Edinburgh anymore,' he said.

'You were a coward and it's not like you,' she said, 'but I didn't come here to start an argument.'

Renée looked away now.

'I missed you,' she said. 'I know what happened. I was there. But you didn't need to walk out on me.'

He supposed that was what he'd done. It had been so difficult to go through each day that he'd felt like standing by the side of the road and hitching to wherever someone might take him. He was still not sure how he had managed to leave in an organized way.

'It was…' he said but did not complete that sentence either. Then the right words occurred to him. 'You're right. I treated you abominably, and I'm sorry.'

Renée's face softened.

'All right,' she said. An expression of guilt swept over her. 'I didn't mean to come here and lay into you. How are you? How have you been?'

'Oh, you know,' Jason said.

'No, I don't. That is why I'm here. I know you told me not to come but I was fed up paying attention to that. I did tell you that – in one of the emails.' The word email was said with contempt.

As Jason looked at her, an image of Isla came into his mind, and confused him. He had been living such a different life up here, and he had stepped into it so quickly. Now that Renée had turned up again, he probed his feelings for her. He hadn't forgotten about her. That much was obvious. Shame stabbed at him. He'd become so obsessed with Isla it had been a betrayal of Renée, there was no doubt about that. Not that he'd slept with Isla.

He'd never even kissed her. But he'd allowed her to possess him. How did he feel about that now? How had it happened anyway? And why did he feel he'd been unfaithful to Renée when he'd already left her?

'What's the school you're working in like?' Renée asked. 'Do you like it?'

That was another difficult question, though Jason didn't suppose it was intended to be.

'I've been dismissed,' Jason said. 'Or they're in the process of it.'

'What? You? But you're God's gift to teaching. You're good anyway. I know that because I've talked to enough people in that school in Edinburgh you taught in. What are they sacking you for?'

'How many hours have you got?' Jason said as he started to work out how to explain.

'All the time it takes,' Renée said.

Her eyes were looking at Jason with an intensity that surprised him.

'What's been going on?' she asked.

'There's been a bit of fuss with parents,' Jason said.

'What about?'

'You've heard about The Poolside Murder? It's been all over the news.'

'Of course. But that can't have anything to do with you.'

It was a shock to realise that someone who'd played such a major part in his life like Renée didn't know anything about what he'd been going through.

'I was there.'

'At Mark Landy's house? Why?'

'I was invited. I'd bumped into a bunch of people at a café on the front, and they asked me.'

'Doesn't sound like you. Go on.'

'I've no idea what happened at the pool. A guy was found dead the next day. That's all I know. But I was there. There were drugs. Some people have been making up stories about it being a sex party as well, though it wasn't. When word got round about all that at school, you can imagine what everyone made of it. Teacher at sex and drug party. Not good for the school's reputation – or mine. Parents were up in arms about what kind of person the school was employing to teach their children.'

'That sounds difficult. But you? Someone must have spoken up for you?'

'As it happens, the headmaster did.'

'Useful.'

'Except they then decided to go after him because he'd backed me, so he had to give up on that.'

'That's bad.'

'And it gets worse.'

'How can it do that?'

'The leader of the parents' group which was gunning for me was a man called Tod McPhail and he's been found murdered.'

'But that doesn't have anything to do with you?'

'What's any of it got to do with me? But the police tell me I have motive. Everybody thinks that.'

'You? Motive?'

Renée looked as if she was having difficulty taking that in.

'But they need to have more than that on you, don't they?' she said. 'After all you didn't do it.'

There was a pause, and it hurt Jason to see doubts starting to form in Renée's face.

'Did you?'

He felt emotions gathering.

'What do you think?' Jason said.

He took a deep breath as he struggled to keep control; he had almost screamed at Renée.

'I can't tell you how bad it is, Renée. Paul Robertson, that's the man who was found dead by the pool. The police think I killed him too.'

'Why?'

'You've no idea what this has been like. The suspicions some people have, the way they judge you without even knowing anything about it. I sometimes think I'm not going to get out of this.'

'Calm down, Jason. Of course you will.' Then, after a long pause, she said, 'I'll help you through it.'

'You will?'

Jason looked at her hard. This was the woman he had left behind because he couldn't face up to things in Edinburgh, and she was there, offering to help him in Nairn.

'Why do the police think you have anything to do with the death of Paul Robertson?'

This was where things became even more problematic. If Jason explained that, he had to explain about Isla.

'You know who Paul Robertson is?'

'Vaguely. Tell me about it again. I didn't pay much attention to that story in the newspapers.'

'He's – or he was – the husband of Isla Landy, Mark Landy's daughter.'

'And the pool belonged to Mark Landy?'

'Yes.'

'Go on.'

'Isla's been really cut up about it. Her husband was murdered. It's what you would expect.'

Renée picked up on something in Jason's expression very quickly.

'Has she been crying on your shoulder? Why?'

'I'd got to know her. I was there.'

'You're a soft enough touch for that. How well did you know her before that?'

There was an edge in her voice as she asked that question.

'We'd only just met,' Jason said.

'And she's clung onto you?'

'Yes.'

'Odd. But never mind. At least you don't have a motive for killing Paul Robertson. Why have they latched onto you as a suspect?'

'People seem to think I was in some sort of relationship with Isla before then.'

'Which she tells them wasn't the case?'

'Of course she does.' He paused. 'I assume.' Why did Renée look disbelieving? 'She will have done.'

Renée's expression became even more thoughtful.

'Would Isla murder her husband?'

'You haven't met her. If you had, you'd know that's ridiculous. She's the sweetest girl.'

'I see. Well, she'd fool you into thinking that.'

'I'm not as gullible as you seem to think. Isla hasn't murdered anybody. She's so cut up about Paul's death. You should see her. And did you know the police had her down at the police station? They had her in for twelve hours while they questioned her. Imagine what that was like for her. She loses her husband and then they treat her like that.'

'Assuming she's innocent it's awful for her, yes, but you don't really know her. You said you'd only just met.'

'I've got to know her well since.'

'Have you?' Renée said.

Jason didn't like the look on Renée's face when she said that.

'She didn't do it. She's incapable of that. She's fragile. She couldn't.'

'Really?'

Renée and Jason looked at each other.

'Not that I've met her,' Renée said. 'I don't suppose I would know.'

'She wouldn't,' Jason said.

'But I do know this much. You've fallen for her and I'm by the wayside,' Renée said.

Jason couldn't bear to see Renée looking as upset as that.

'It's good to see you again, Renée, really, it is.'

'Are there any more women you're keeping round here I should know about?'

She'd only just turned up, and he'd lost her again. That was what the look on her face said now. He shouldn't still have feelings for Renée, considering those he'd been developing for Isla but, now that he'd met up with Renée again, he'd discovered that he did. It was as if his two separate existences were merging in an uncomfortable way. He didn't know what he was doing – about anything.

'I'm so pleased to see you again, Renée,' Jason said.

He was but he noticed his mind was probing a surprising line of thought. If things didn't work out with Isla, he could have Renée back. And if things didn't work out with Renée, he could have Isla. When had he become as cold as that?

'Just as well you said that,' Renée said. 'But, to be practical, what's happening with the police?'

'They had me in for questioning.'

'They didn't keep you in, obviously.'

'But they'll keep probing. They like me for this.'

'You're going to need a lawyer then.'

'Mark Landy's offered to pay for one for me.'

'He must think a lot of you to be offering to do that. How close have you been getting to Isla?'

'She needs someone. Mark knows I'm trying to be there for her. As a friend. That's all.'

'Very good,' Renée said. Then she said it again, 'Very good.' But the expression on her face said she didn't think so.

'Just what do you know about these people? Not much. They're rich, which means they come from an entirely different world to the one you do. You don't understand anything about the way they think, so they could be up to anything, and it would go straight past you.'

'Or not,' Jason said. 'They're still people. It's good of Mark to offer to help.'

There was a look of concentration on Renée's face.

'Jason,' she said. 'If Mark Landy pays for a lawyer for you, who does the lawyer answer to?'

Jason gave that thought, then shrugged his shoulders. If Renée ever met Mark Landy, she would know that was nothing to worry about.

NINETEEN

Jason found himself meeting with Andy McAulay in The Bandstand once more, which was Andy's idea, not his. Andy said he wanted to compare notes – again. Jason did wonder about Andy and meetings. It felt as if there was something scheming about them – or maybe Jason was being defensive in thinking that.

They sat with tumblers of amber liquid in front of them, beside a warm fire, and Jason tried to relax, but found it difficult. He could see that there was tension inside Andy. As Andy sat there in silence, Jason could sense he was building up to something – what he wanted to ask, Jason supposed. Then Andy did start talking.

'When was that guy Tod killed again?'

'When you and I were sitting talking together – right here,' Jason replied.

'Which means it wasn't you.'

'Definitely.'

'How do they know what time he died?'

Jason puzzled over that one.

'You'd have to ask them,' was all he said in reply.

'Do you watch much crime?' Andy asked.

'Police dramas on TV? Why? What have they got to do with what happened to Tod?'

'They use real police methods.'

'Apparently,' Jason said.

'Police always ask pathologists for a precise time of death, and do you know the reply they get? Time of death is the one thing they can't be precise about. Cause of death? Yes. In endless detail. When someone died. No.'

'What are you saying here exactly? I could have done it – at a different time, and be using you as an alibi?'

'It would be possible. Is that what you're doing?'

'No. I'm not.'

Jason was furious. What kind of person was Andy McAulay? But it would do no good to berate him, Jason supposed.

'I didn't kill Tod,' he said.

But as he looked at Andy, he could see Andy didn't believe him.

'I don't want to give an alibi for someone who did a murder,' Andy said.

'That isn't what you've been doing,' Jason said, 'and you've already given your evidence. You and I were sitting here talking at the time you said – which we were. What's the problem with that?'

'If the police decide I'm giving you a false alibi, where does that leave me?'

'Have they?' Jason asked.

'They could, and I don't want to be in that position. No one else but you has a motive for killing Tod McPhail.'

'You've decided on that shaky basis it was me? Thanks very much. You're wrong. You do know that, don't you?'

'Someone killed him, and the police have already grilled me about Paul's death, because I'm a suspect for that in their eyes. If they decide I'm lying about your alibi, that puts me in a bad position. I hardly know you at all. I do know you've killed someone before, that Eddie whatever his name was.'

'Look at me,' Jason said.

He was finding it difficult staying calm now. Andy stared back at him.

'What?' he said.

'Do I look like a murderer to you?'

But, as Andy returned his stare, Jason could see that he did.

'Isla's someone we've all been friends with for years,' Andy said. 'We know her. I can see why you've become so fond of her – and she is vulnerable. Anyone might want to protect her. Is that why you killed Paul – because you were trying to look out for her?'

'Get real,' Jason replied, his voice now sharp and exasperated. 'Apart from anything else, I'd only just got to know her.'

'So you say, but you hadn't just met her, had you?'

'That's tosh,' Jason said. He could have hit Andy because of that comment, but fortunately didn't.

'What spoils your story is you couldn't stay away from her, could you? Which made it obvious to everybody how well you did know her.'

Jason felt defeated by the determined look on Andy's face. Arguments were not going to work on him.

'Isla would melt anyone's heart,' Andy went on. 'And she is easily hurt. She doesn't have to act that. You should have seen her when she had that breakdown after her cousin's accident. That was tragic, a dreadful thing to happen to Isla.'

'And Paul's death's difficult for her,' Jason said.

Andy knocked back his whisky.

'I shouldn't be seen with you,' he said. 'It makes me look guilty too.'

He walked away. Then he turned back.

'We all have to look out for ourselves.'

As he continued walking, Jason was left wondering what Andy meant by that, and feeling sure it didn't bode well.

Questions turned in his mind. Who murdered Tod McPhail? And who killed Paul Robertson? Were they thinking of murdering anyone else any time soon? Like him? Though why anyone would want to do that, he couldn't imagine.

The most likely thing to happen would be that he would take the blame for what had happened already — unless he could find a way to avoid it.

TWENTY

Then Renée was back at him, so quickly, with a barrage of questions and comments — all about Isla. He ought to have known she'd have more to say.

'Have you been sleeping with her? You've had your arm round her to comfort her? I'm supposed to believe that's it? I've seen her now. Why's she interested in you? If she is, something's up.'

Renée hadn't even been giving him the chance to answer as she'd made up her mind. Jason was disappointed in her; he hadn't thought her so jealous.

'She's just a nice girl,' Jason said.

'A girl who looks like that? Get real. She's known how to twist men round her little finger since she was four.'

Jason thought that was unfair.

'I know, Renée. I shouldn't have left you the way I did. It was bad. I'm sorry.'

'I'll say it was bad. I still haven't worked out what I did wrong.'

'You didn't — it wasn't about that.'

'So, what was it about?'

'It— It wasn't you. It was me.'

'That cliché.'

'But it was.'

'Have you any idea what it was like? You protect me from an evil monster like that, so I feel I owe you one big time, and then you walk out on me! Where did you think that left me?'

'I did a bit more than protect you. I killed him.'

'It's not your fault he chose the wrong angle to fall at and hit a marble tabletop. Would you stop blaming yourself for that?'

Renée's arguments were coming one on top of the other fast and Jason was feeling overwhelmed, particularly as he had never told Renée about the deliberate trip on Eddie. It had been a confusing scene and even Renée hadn't seen it. When she told him to stop blaming himself for that, she didn't know how much he had been to blame. He asked himself why he'd been able to tell Isla when he couldn't tell Renée. Perhaps it was because he'd done it for her.

'How on earth am I supposed to do that?' He was yelling now. 'And should I? I'm even glad I killed him, and he can't come after you again. Have you any idea how that feels? Not that it's got anything to do with what's going on here. I don't know who I am anymore. And I can't live with myself.'

But Renée's tirade continued.

'He was a bastard and I'm glad you killed him. Why didn't you stay with me, and we could have been glad about it together? And felt bad about it if we wanted to — together?'

Then she stopped yelling at him, and Jason found himself looking into eyes with an appeal in them that cut through him. Her voice became soft and quiet.

'I did see you trip him,' she said.

'What?'

'I saw the move you did to lever him over.'

'You saw that?'

'Yes.'

'You didn't say anything.'

'I knew why you had to keep quiet about that, so I did too. Good for you. And you got him – that was good too?' Renée said.

He felt so inadequate in the face of Renée's certainty and there was something about it that made him feel glad, but there was also something wrong in what Renée was saying. Wasn't there?

'Basically... no. I killed him. It wasn't good.'

'But it was still an accident. Go a bit easier on yourself. You killed someone because of me. I owe it to you to help you through that.'

Jason was glad Renée felt like that. It proved something about her – she had genuine feelings for him, which he should have been able to guess just from the fact she'd turned up in Nairn – though he didn't know how to respond to it. He'd wondered about her at the time. He'd thought Renée might just have been using him to help her get away from Eddie. It had felt as if she knew how to manipulate him too well. He looked at her in silence. He had misjudged this woman – and he hadn't treated her fairly.

Then Renée asked, 'What did any of it have to do with running away to Nairn?'

How did he reply to that?

'I don't know. I just couldn't continue staying in Edinburgh.'

'Which I still don't get.'

'I couldn't live with what I'd done.'

'You survived the court case. You didn't go to prison. What was there to run away from?'

'Myself?'

Why didn't Renée understand that when it was so obvious?

'Exactly how do you do that by teaching in the Highlands?'

As the next sentence forced itself out, it left him almost in physical pain.

'I almost threw myself off the Walter Scott monument. I mean it. I paid for a ticket, walked all the way to the top, and stood there for about ten minutes trying to find the courage to throw myself off. And I couldn't even do that. Have you any idea how ashamed I am for not having the courage to do it?'

That stopped Renée in her tracks but not for long. Now sympathy gushed out.

'Thank God you didn't. Jason, you didn't really think of committing suicide, did you? Why didn't you tell me? It's awful. You're not thinking of doing anything like that again, are you?'

What a thing that had been to confess to. But he had.

'If I'd been going to, I would have done it.'

'Crisis moment passed?'

Jason looked carefully at her as he considered the question.

'Yes,' he said.

'If you ever think of doing anything like that again, you will let me know, won't you? Right?'

The smile she gave him was warm. For a moment it felt like the warmest thing he'd ever experienced, and the sympathy suddenly felt almost overwhelming.

'You were all on your own, weren't you?' she said.

'I suppose,' he said.

'And you have been for so long – since your mother died. You'd been brought up just by her and then you lost her. And I've let you down.'

Ah, Jason thought. The other thing he never talked about, his mother's death.

'Cancer,' he said.

'It could happen to anyone, and it had to happen to her.'

'It was a couple of years ago now,' he said.

As if that made much difference.

'And you strike out on your own by leaving Edinburgh for Nairn when you meet up with a crisis. That wasn't the best idea you ever had.'

Renée stood just looking at him for a while, and Jason had difficulty in keeping her gaze.

'You never did get me, did you?' she said.

'What do you mean?'

'I wasn't just clinging onto you to get away from Eddie. I love you, you chump.'

That was something to take in. He tried to explain himself to her further.

'I thought of standing by the side of the road, putting out my thumb, and letting the road take me where it would. I almost did that. It would have been easy enough. That wouldn't have taken physical courage. But there was something about it that didn't appeal either. The uncertainty, I think. I did succeed in escaping though. I even managed it in a semi-organized way. I got myself a job in Nairn and disappeared up here, which I discussed with you at the time. I'm sorry it meant leaving you behind.'

His thinking had seemed clear at the time, but, as Renée said she really loved him, had it been?

'I thought that was crazy then and still do,' Renée told him. 'Running away from everyone – to be miserable all by yourself up here – how did that make sense? Did you not think I might have wanted to help you through all that? Don't you think I felt guilty about what you did for me?'

If she loved him, she would have done. He'd been a fool.

'Was I thinking? I don't know. I was feeling, mostly desperation, and I didn't think I deserved you.'

'Selfish bastard. Didn't it occur to you I might have needed someone to help me through things?'

That too. Yes. He should have realised that.

'It does now. Yes.'

Jason was gaping at Renée helplessly. His words had run out and he hadn't explained himself. What he had done didn't make any sense to him anymore, so no, Renée would never get it, and she had made him feel guilty for not being there for her.

'It was beginning to work, escaping up here,' he said, still feeling the need to defend himself desperately, though his excuse sounded feeble to him. He looked helplessly at Renée.

'Till someone else turned up dead,' he added. 'That happens a lot near me.'

'But it doesn't have anything to do with you. How do you know it wasn't your precious Isla who murdered Paul?'

'You're jealous of her.'

Renée made no attempt to apologise for that.

'What else would I be? But it doesn't make any difference. And how do you know it wasn't her?'

He thought Renée was being grossly unfair there. He was in no man's land between them, wasn't he? Isla was being friendly and helping me fit in here, find friends, and settle. It's not her fault someone killed her husband.'

'You really don't think it could have been her?'

That accusation again. Jason laughed, and it was a bitter laugh, which he didn't like. He was beginning to realise how jealous Renée was of Isla, and he didn't like seeing that.

'She didn't do it,' he said. 'She told me. She's not even the sort of person who would. She's warm, generous – and loving. It's not in her nature.'

'As if you'd be able to see through her. You've never been able to see through anyone I've introduced you to.'

'That's not true. Why do you have to underestimate me like that?'

'You don't even get my feelings for you right now.'

She was wrong about that, he was getting those – and he'd thought himself in love with Renée at one time, which left him exactly where now? He'd left, met Isla, and become fascinated with her, which left him not deserving Renée. He knew that much. But he wondered again what his affections were for Renée now. When he thought about it, his emotions had become a bit of a mystery generally to him lately. It was like probing under ice trying to explore them, as if cold calculations had taken over his life since Eddie died and lay between him and his very soul. But he was feeling the need to take Renée in his arms now, even though there was still Isla to defend. All that conflict was something to cope with.

'You've got Isla wrong. She isn't what you think.'

It was the wrong thing to say, and Jason should have known that. Renée stood up and made for the door. She reached it quickly and was soon on the other side of it, closing it behind her firmly. Jason doubted if it would be opened again any time soon. One thing stood out in his mind from his two conversations with Renée. There were feelings between them, but they hadn't ended up in each other's arms.

TWENTY-ONE

The police turned up after that. Jason was having quite a day. When he opened the door after a thunderous knocking, he found himself confronted by a stern-looking Inspector Buchanan and Sergeant Ruthven. Memories of his arrest after the death of Eddie Caldwell came back to him: unforgiving looks from uniformed men with long arms and handcuffs; the horror of the seriousness of what he'd done; the weakness in his limbs as he'd allowed himself to be led along. At least the handcuffs weren't out this time – yet.

Not that there was any beating about the bush. Nor were there any careful probing questions. There was just an authoritative statement.

'I'm arresting you under Section 1 of the Criminal Justice Act 2016 on suspicion of the murders of Paul Robertson and Tod McPhail – as keeping you in custody is necessary to bring you to court. Do you understand?'

Jason certainly did. He wished that he didn't. He nodded his head. Buchanan continued in the same phlegmatic way.

'You are not obliged to say anything but anything you do say will be noted and may be used in evidence. You have the right of access to a solicitor. Your rights will be further explained to you at the police station where you will be required to state your name, date of birth, place of birth, nationality and address.'

Buchanan had certainly got it all off pat. The stilted phrases were ones that he had to parrot out, Jason supposed – to make sure he left Jason no way out. Then Ruthven did have the bracelets out and Jason had to hold out his hands. After all the talking and wondering that had been going on, his arrest felt sudden and unexpected. They led him down the stairs into the car park where a police car was waiting. One of the rear doors was opened and he was pushed in.

There wasn't a large crowd to watch his demise, which was a relief, but there were a couple of people looking out of windows. His arrest had not gone unnoticed. Jessie had her eagle eyes fixed on him. Jessie was old and retired and did not have many interests in life that he knew of, so had plenty of time to notice everything that was going on. She would be pleased something was happening in her day that was different to housework and her TV shows. And there was Eck at another window. He was a bit bleary-eyed-looking, but then his life did occur at odd times. He must be getting ready to go on a shift. At least this would wake him properly.

The police car pulled out and Jason was driven to the station. He didn't allow himself to look through the windows as he didn't want to see the questioning eyes of anyone else he might know.

When he reached the station, he was processed – as he supposed it was called – by a sergeant, then led to an interview room and told to sit down. He was left to himself. In the room was a desk with a recorder, and some chairs. The walls were grey concrete, and the floor was covered in grey linoleum. Jason thought wryly that would all be easily cleaned after blood was spilled. He told himself not to be so gloomy, but it was a cheerless enough room, as was his situation. The one narrow window did not help. It allowed neither light nor air. As Jason sat there, he wondered what proof they could have assembled against him – because they would have some.

Then Buchanan and Ruthven entered the room and sat themselves down on chairs opposite him. They looked relaxed as if deliberately putting across the message this was no skin off their noses. Buchanan carried a file which he laid on the table in front of him.

'We're now going to question you about the murders,' he said. 'Do you want a solicitor present?'

Jason had been thinking about that. That's what a habitual criminal would do, he thought, hide behind a lawyer, which was why he was inclined not to. He didn't want to make himself look more guilty than he already did. He thought the reaction of an innocent person might be to think he didn't need a solicitor as he'd done nothing wrong so couldn't have anything to worry about.

On the other hand, Jason didn't know the legalities of the situation he was in so it might be sensible to ask for a solicitor, but this had come at Jason so fast he was feeling overpowered by it and in a strange mood. He felt inclined to resign himself to his fate. There was also that feeling of disbelief. How could this be happening?

He would wait to see what evidence they came up with. Then he would know how serious this was and could decide to use a lawyer if he wanted to.

The recorder was switched on and Buchanan spoke into it to establish the interview situation that was unfolding, and the people present. Jason looked anxiously at him as he waited for whatever was about to happen. Buchanan's face remained worryingly unworried.

'Regarding your relationship with Tod McPhail, how would you describe it?'

An easy enough question to start off with, Jason thought.

'He was the father of a pupil I taught, Allie McPhail.'

'Would you say you got on with him?'

Buchanan could be expected to want to know that, and Jason had better be honest. Everyone already knew the answer anyway.

'I didn't. He was the chairman of the parents' group. He was concerned about the fact I was teaching in the school, and he said he was in the middle of orchestrating my dismissal. There was a rumour going around that I might be a murderer. Can't think where they might have got that idea from.'

'Did he have the meeting with you on his own?'

'Yes. He turned up at the end of the day.'

'How did you react to that?'

'I attempted to defend myself.'

'Were you very angry?'

'I was annoyed obviously, but he was a parent. I stayed polite.'

'We have a witness who says that he heard raised voices at the time and that you were furious and expressed this freely.'

'Who said that?' Jason asked. 'Because that's tosh.'

Buchanan didn't reply, just continued with his questions.

'You have no alibi for the time of Tod's murder?'

'Yes, I do. We've gone over this. I was with Andy McAulay.'

'Who has withdrawn the statement saying he was with you.'

'Has he really?'

So Andy had gone through with that. Thanks, Andy.

'Can he do that? He's already made a statement and signed it.'

'There was confusion about the time.'

'How convenient. And how do you know there still isn't?'

'In any case, you now have no solid alibi. Unless you can come up with another one.'

'I was with Andy. That's not something I've "come up" with.'

'That doesn't hold water, which doesn't help you.'

But Jason was thinking that this couldn't be all the evidence: an overheard argument in a public place, a school; and an inability to establish where he was at the time of Tod's death. He waited to see what else Buchanan would come up with.

'We have physical proof that places you at the scene of the murder.'

Buchanan opened his file and pushed a piece of paper towards Jason.

'As you can see there are fibres from a foreign source that were found there. And when the fibre was analysed it was found to contain traces of your DNA, Mr Sutherland. Can you give me any explanation for how that could have occurred?'

Jason stared at the evidence sheet. He hadn't murdered Tod McPhail so he hadn't been at the murder scene. He didn't see how they could have DNA linking him to the site. Yet the sheet did say fibres from a jacket had been found, and he could be sure the police would be searching his flat right now for the jacket. This could get worse.

But he wasn't sure how the evidence was possible. He had met up with Tod McPhail but that had been at school. Maybe fibres had transferred themselves to Tod then. They had shaken hands. Tod did have that excessively firm handshake of the over-assertive. It had been difficult to pull himself away from it. That could explain it. Jason presented the explanation to Buchanan who looked unimpressed.

'Then there's the murder method,' Buchanan said.

'Which was?' Jason said.

'He was hit with a blunt instrument on the back of the head. And the place of contact fits you.'

'You're joking,' Jason said. 'How could that fit me?'

'You know how sensitive that area of the skull is. It's the same area that did for Eddie Caldwell whom you did kill.'

'Accidentally.'

'Apparently. But, in any case, a learning experience.'

'I was defending someone then. There's no comparison between the incidents.'

'But you were defending yourself against Mr McPhail. You said he was orchestrating your dismissal from your job.'

'But you must have thought I waited for him deliberately that night. That's cold-blooded. That's not how Eddie Caldwell was killed. He died in an accident because of something that happened at the time. The way Tod was murdered – that's not me, and I didn't do it.'

'There's motive, physical evidence, and opportunity. You could have been there. There's no proof you were anywhere else.'

'It's all a bit circumstantial, surely?'

That didn't convince Buchanan either.

'Then there's the murder of Paul Robertson,' he went on. 'You can't deny being at the pool party. There are too many people who place you there.'

'I was there, yes, but so were a lot of others.'

'You're Isla's lover.'

'No. I'm not.'

'There are a lot of witnesses to a relationship between you.'

'We're friends.'

'You had the motivation and the opportunity. There was no witness to the murder but plenty to the fact you were in a drunken state. The fact you can't remember anything about the party shows that too.'

'This is tosh. I'd only just met Isla and Paul. I had no reason to kill him.'

'We have a statement from Isla about your relationship with her.'

'What?'

'She's admitted to us that you and she were lovers and from long before the pool party.'

'No. I don't believe she said that.'

Buchanan didn't even bother repeating it. Isla wouldn't say any of that so what was going on?

'We have a full statement from her. She didn't see you doing the murder, but she did see you arguing with him – about her.'

'No. She didn't. She couldn't have said that.'

There was something wrong here.

'You can deny it as much as you like but we believe her. You must have killed Paul is the conclusion anyone would draw from what she said. Then you tried to conceal your crime by making it look as if it was a drugs and alcohol induced drowning.'

Jason was feeling apoplectic now, if helpless.

'But none of this happened,' he said, and he didn't know why it didn't come out as a scream. It was more like a whisper.

'Isla says she felt sorry for you which was why she tried to help you cover up. She felt partly responsible because you did it to protect her. She wishes she'd never told you about her argument with Paul that evening when Paul lashed out with his fist. She knows about your previous court case, when you killed Eddie Caldwell in a quarrel over a woman – to protect her – and it was obvious that was what you'd done again. You killed Paul to protect Isla. She'd stayed friends with you after that because she couldn't believe in her heart of hearts that you'd meant to do it, though it was the second time you'd done such a thing. And then there was the business of Tod McPhail. That confirmed it for her. When she'd finished thinking that through, that was when she came to us.'

Jason had been listening with fascination but mostly horror. And now that Buchanan had paused, he finally had the chance to speak again.

'She's inventive. I give her credit for that. If two-faced. But you can't believe any of this. Can you?'

Buchanan continued.

'You've already been told you're under arrest. You will be held in custody for twelve hours while we assemble further proof from the search of your flat and devices, during which time you will be submitted to questioning. After that you will be charged.'

Buchanan's implacable face stared at him. The look held Jason as if in a vice. He was stunned.

'It would save a lot of everyone's time if you admitted this.'

That woke Jason's brain cells up again. He'd made up his mind now about that solicitor. He needed one. Buchanan strongly suggested a confession again as he said this was only going to end up one way, but he told Jason a lawyer would be arranged. Jason decided against using Mark Landy's and opted for a duty solicitor instead. He didn't know what was going on here. Isla had been speaking against him. Did that mean Mark was in on this?

Then he was taken to a cell.

He was still incredulous. He couldn't believe the lies Isla had told. She'd said he was her lover! He'd have liked that, but it hadn't happened, which he'd thought was because his relationship with Isla had something good and noble in it, above the physical. Maybe on his side that had been the case.

She'd enthralled him. That was probably the word. He'd been fascinated – with the way the back of her neck curved; with the cut of her hair, the infectiousness of her smile, and the tears that sometimes coursed down her face; with the scent she used; with the way she spoke; with the clarity in her eyes; with the genuineness in her – that hadn't even been there. He'd wanted to reach out and help her through her difficulties. He'd helped her all right – to set himself up to take the blame for Paul's death; and Tod's. That could only be because she'd done the murders. What else was there to think?

Now he had to work out what he should do. How could he react to any of this? And did he really know where he was as a person? He was like a jigsaw made up of pieces from different puzzles. Who was this person that Isla and the police were talking about? Who was this short-tempered killer called Jason Sutherland? He wasn't the same person he'd always known himself to be.

In a way, yes. He got it. It was how he'd seen himself after the death of Eddie Caldwell. But Paul and Tod's deaths? What was going on there?

He still had no clear recollection of the party, which didn't help. But he hadn't killed Paul, as Isla said he had. Then a niggling thought came. Or had he? He couldn't remember anything about that night. He did know he hadn't killed Tod McPhail – unless there was something seriously wrong with his memory. But if he hadn't, who had? Who else might want Tod dead? Had he started suffering from periodic blackouts? A psychiatrist had examined him after Eddie's death. That was something that had been arranged by the police. And something the psychiatrist said had been odd. Something about an emotional disconnect between himself and other people. He was surprised to be released after that. The psychiatrist had suggested he was capable of being involved in events such as those again.

TWENTY-TWO

Next, Jason found himself in actual prison, awaiting the processing of his case. When he was told there was a visitor for him, he didn't expect it to be Isla, but there she was, waiting behind the glass partition that stood between prison visitors and prisoners. He sat opposite and looked at her through the grille that allowed them to talk to each other. He couldn't quite make out what the expression was on her face, couldn't make up his mind whether it was triumph or worry or some odd mixture. His heart still missed a beat when he saw her, not that he knew what to say. She had betrayed him. He could start with that but didn't. He sat in silence, waiting to see what was going to unfold.

Isla was playing with a lock of her hair, and Jason wondered how she could look so demure in a place like this. Then her face opened into one of her smiles. It was the one that opened like a flower – of the well-cultivated variety. The violet eyes blazed, the smile wide, the teeth as white as always. Genuineness and kindness were on her face, but Jason didn't believe either now.

'So, they arrested you?' she said. 'The British police. What can I say?'

Jason tried to control his reaction, but his anger must have been clear.

'They've assembled a case strong enough to convince a jury – so they tell me. And if they can find anything else on my phone, computer, or in my flat, they'll use that too. Though after the testimony you gave, I doubt if they'll need any more,' Jason replied.

Isla said nothing at first.

Then she said, 'How bad is it in here?'

'It's a prison,' Jason said. 'Things can't get any worse.'

'I'm sorry.'

'Are you? I hate to mention it, but as well as saying you saw me arguing with Paul that night, you said we'd been lovers, which we hadn't. And we'd only just met when he died.'

Isla turned on her smile again. Jason wondered why she bothered.

'You wanted to be my lover though.'

'What?'

Jason looked at her in disbelief.

'What has "wanted to be" got to do with it?' he said. 'And aren't you assuming a lot?'

'It's got everything to do with it, don't you think?'

Now the smile had a seriousness to it that was unnerving – before kindness returned.

'You "wanted" to kill Eddie. You admitted that. And you tripped him. You got away with one there.'

The gentleness in her voice floored Jason.

'What?' he said.

'Darling,' Isla said, and now she sounded like an adult talking to a child. 'It's who you are.'

'What is?'

'You kill people.'

'Eddie's death was an accident.'

'According to the court, but you've always known differently. That's why you've never been able to live with Eddie's death. Because you were so glad when you found

143

out he was dead you could have done it again. You're a murderer at heart whatever the court decided. You said so yourself. You're dangerous. Don't you think you ought to be volunteering to take the fall for something to make the world a safer place?'

An odd sort of logic, Jason thought. Did Isla really think that?

'I didn't kill Paul. And I didn't kill Tod.'

'So you say. You did kill Eddie Caldwell and you were lucky to get away with that one.'

Now the kind smile seemed to have slipped into something else and Jason recognized it; it was the smile her father used in his movies when he was moving in for the kill, and it hit Jason right in the stomach.

'Who would want to go down for something they didn't do?' he said.

Then her smile changed again, and became soothing, like the expression on the face of a nurse or some Mary Poppins-like character – innocent, self-righteous, angelic. And her voice was reassuring.

'You wanted to kill Eddie Caldwell. You know you did. That's why you felt the way you did afterwards. And you're a complete mess because of that. You need to make amends. Don't you want to heal? To become whole again? You wanted to kill him, just as you wanted to make love to me. I said you had, that's all. What's the difference? Not that much really. You say you didn't kill Paul, but you must have wanted to when you discovered how he treated me. Just as you wanted to kill Eddie because of the way he treated Renée. And with so much wanting to do things going on inside you, you must have wanted to kill Tod McPhail as well. How does anyone know you didn't do either of those murders? You do want to make the world a safer place, don't you? And you do want to make amends, don't you? You know you do. And now that you've been arrested you will. You'll come to thank me, Jason.'

144

Jason's mouth must have been wide open. What else would it have been? His eyes did not leave Isla's face.

Isla was such a fresh-faced young woman and had such a sense of fun; she had a simpering giggle that was contagious – and a raucous laugh; she filled every moment with her sheer exuberance; her bubbly nature flowed effortlessly through her, with that simpering giggle and that sense of fun, Isla, she of the golden looks and the glamorous film world background. But, listening to that piece of logic, she was also insane – or was he the one who was crazy?

Isla said nothing now, she just gazed at him as if what she had told Jason was simple and obvious. He only had to think a bit harder to see the sense of it. The words played themselves in Jason's mind. Over and over. Step into my logic, said the spider to the fly. And where had that last thought come from?

Then Jason found himself thinking of Eddie's body on the bar-room floor, and the forlorn way it had lain, spreadeagled there after that surprisingly short fall; he thought of the anger and life there had been in Eddie just a moment before when he had been yelling at Renée. Eddie had told her she belonged to him, and then nothing had belonged to him except the space he lay in.

Eddie had no right to insist Renée was still his after she had decided to leave him. But there had been energy in the way he had argued, and then, one moment later, there was none in him, and the angry eyes held nothing. Jason thought again about what Isla had said. That reasoning was bizarre, but could there be any sense in it?

Isla's eyes had continued to smile at him; they were alive, and they poured bucketloads of sympathy in his direction. The upturn at the corners of her lips tantalised.

'You need to confess, Jason. You need to face up to guilt and pay a penalty. It's the only way you're going to move on. Take your chance to do that.'

He must have been feeling desperate. Isla was beginning to sound reasonable.

TWENTY-THREE

Then Jason was back on his bunk in his prison cell, gazing at a blank wall. He had been depressed before seeing Isla. Now he felt as if a giant weight was pressing on him.

Jason shared the cell with someone, a young man called Tommy, a skinny person with a shaven head, scraggy beard, and pale, unhealthy-looking skin. Tommy did not talk much, as he appeared to be terrified of Jason, which was fair enough as Jason was on remand for murder. When Tommy did speak, the voice was guttural, the tone low, the words enunciated with a lack of effort and apparent interest. It was a wonder they cleared his beard. Silence seemed to suit him better. His eyes held an inward look to them as if he'd buried himself somewhere inside, lost in whatever depressing thoughts he was having.

Tommy had a cocaine problem. He had gone to meet his dealer one night, which was when he'd been arrested. He'd met him in the car park at Inverness Railway Station, and had been about to take him to Dingwall, where Tommy could introduce the dealer to other drug users. They'd been stopped en route by a police car, and both had been arrested. Tommy had professed innocence. He wasn't the drug dealer, which was true. He was just after cocaine. But he had committed a crime. He'd been transporting drugs and was complicit in their being sold to users, for which he'd been put in prison for a couple of years which he thought was a bit much. He'd just been after some gear and look at what had happened.

He and Jason had got on fine at first – until he'd discovered what Jason was in for. Then Tommy had clammed up, being terrified of him. Jason had sympathy for Tommy over that, though he felt even sorrier for himself. Despite his denials, Tommy had committed a crime, and Jason hadn't done what he was accused of – as far as he knew. Then again, after Eddie Caldwell's death, he could hardly claim to be any paragon. And Isla's words wouldn't leave him.

Jason thought back to what life had been like since Eddie died. He had thought to lift that dreadful mood of his with a change of scene. He'd thought he'd seen a real chance of doing that in Nairn if he could have managed to join that group of casual people he'd so admired when he'd watched them relaxing at the café on the front.

There had been something too about Nairn itself, that outlook over the firth, the cheerfulness of the people who'd thronged along its shore to chatter and waft ice creams and cartons of chips about. He remembered looking at someone paddle-boarding off the shore on a calm sea and thinking now that was it: that expressed everything he wanted – that sense of ease and freedom as light sparkled from the water and a blue sky beckoned.

Yes. After he'd arrived in Nairn, he'd thought he'd caught glimpses in himself of a better mood. Then things had changed as death had returned; it had felt like a curse he could not escape. Those dark feelings of depression had returned; they were like shackles holding him in their grip.

Paul was killed – by someone. Jason had no clear memories of that night so that he could have done it for all that he knew. He had vague memories of a quarrel, pictures of different people who might have been arguing with anyone, and not much idea of what were real memories and what were his imagination. He didn't even know if he'd been involved in an argument himself. He wished he knew that. Had he been furious because Paul had treated Isla badly, and struck Paul? As he couldn't remember what had occurred that night, it could have happened.

Jason did know he hadn't killed Tod because he had that alibi with Andy, though it was a pity Andy had withdrawn it. On the other hand, as Andy had suggested, the police could have been wrong about time of death though he hoped they weren't that amateurish these days. Anyway, he would surely have remembered doing that murder, so how could they have evidence that proved he'd done it? But they said they did. Perhaps he did suffer from blackouts when he could be doing anything and not remember it. That was a depressing thought. He felt as low now as he ever had. He was doubting his own mind. How had he come to this?

Jason was going to be tried and probably found guilty of these murders. Isla had been trying to persuade him to confess. Perhaps he would be given a lighter sentence if he did that. That could be a sensible reason for making a confession.

What about Isla's reasoning? He'd been in the grip of this low mood for so long now it felt as if it were strangling the life out of him; it was certainly squashing his ability to think clearly.

He'd got away with murder – in his own mind, and, as Isla had explained, it was as good as. Did he deserve to be found guilty of something? Would that help him heal? That was a stupid thought, surely. Nothing could do that.

But should he just get this over with and make a confession? He looked around him at the bareness of his cell, which seemed to echo the emptiness inside himself. There was a need to do something about that.

TWENTY-FOUR

But he never did feel low enough to admit to the crimes, which was just as well, because suddenly he was released – just like that – which was a shock.

When he was led from his cell and his things were returned to him, it was explained that the Procurator Fiscal had decided there was not enough evidence to be confident of securing a conviction. Jason wondered how often that happened. The police must have been desperate to get him and assembled their case in too much of a hurry. All that cool confidence in the interview room must have been a front, which was why the attempt to get him to confess. Everyone seemed to want him to do that.

Jason supposed he'd been released because the COPFS hadn't found the DNA evidence convincing, which was why the proof wasn't good enough. Jason had wondered about it. Did it really prove he'd been at the scene of the crime or just in Tod's company at some time? Jason had mixed feelings about his release: he was glad to be out of prison, but he wasn't being exonerated.

Jason found himself standing outside the prison looking around him and wondering how to get home. Not having any reason to, Jason had never visited Inverness prison before. But Inverness is not a big place, and it did not take long for Jason to find his bearings.

Once he was in his flat in Nairn, he made coffee, and collapsed on his settee. Whilst he tried to come to terms with what had just happened, Jason heard a knock on his door. It was a police constable, but not one he had met before.

'Just to let you know, sir, you shouldn't travel anywhere. We may need you for further inquiries.'

Jason was surprised he would turn up just to say that. Perhaps he was checking Jason had returned to his flat.

'You might? Shouldn't you be investigating other people as well? You are doing that, aren't you? Perhaps the reason you haven't enough evidence on me is I didn't do it?'

Jason's patience had worn thin.

'I can't share lines of inquiry with you, sir.'

'I was locked up in prison on a murder charge – on the flimsiest of evidence. I'd like some reassurance here. I'd prefer an apology, but I expect that's too much to ask for.'

'I'm not in charge of the investigation so am not privy to everything that's going on.'

'Have you any idea what I've been going through?' Jason said. 'It was complete hell being in that cell. Do you know what it's like to lose your freedom?'

'You have it now, sir.'

'To an extent. I take it going on a holiday to the Caribbean is out of the question?'

'I'm sorry, sir.'

The policeman turned to go.

'And thanks for the sympathy,' Jason found himself saying to a retreating back. 'The genuineness of it touches the heart.'

The constable's face had been expressionless throughout, and Jason supposed it was no different now.

'But I did do it,' Jason felt like saying for the hell of it but didn't. It wouldn't be worth the shock value.

Once the door had closed behind the policeman, Jason was left to lick his wounds. He sipped his coffee. For once he felt he could do with a drink but there was none in the flat.

A different thought occurred. Renée. It would cheer him up seeing her again. Things had not been good when they parted but she had come all the way to Nairn to see him. He didn't suppose he should bother her after the way he'd treated her – he'd been a rat – but in a way she had been the one who'd got him into his difficulties in the first place. If it hadn't been for her relationship with Eddie, he'd never have been in a scuffle with him. The trouble he found himself in here in Nairn wasn't her fault, but dammit, didn't she owe him something? On reflection, probably not, but he still took out his phone – thank God they'd returned that – and scrolled through his contacts till he came to her name. His thumb swithered over it. Then he rang her.

Her phone rang, then cut to her answer machine. After he'd put his mobile down, he sipped more coffee, realised he was muttering to himself, then forced himself to stop. Maybe he could look her up.

Would she still be in Nairn? Where had she said she'd been staying? The West End Hotel. She had probably gone back down south by now; she hadn't visited him in prison. Maybe no one had told her he'd been arrested though he couldn't believe she'd been unaware of it. He'd have been famous for the day – in the local newspaper at least. It was a pity she hadn't visited him. He'd have enjoyed that.

He rang the West End Hotel to be told by reception she'd checked out days before. He sipped more coffee and pulled a face. He didn't even make good coffee. He never had. He got up from his settee and started pacing the room, decided that was silly, grabbed his coat, and strode out. He made his way to the seafront.

It was afternoon and a grey breezy day. As he strode along the front, he glowered at the waves scudding along. He didn't dare look at the people he passed. He didn't want to talk to them, and he didn't want to answer questions about what he'd been going through. Then he found himself staring at the beach as if looking for meaning in it.

He supposed he ought to be glad he'd been released, but he was in the foulest of moods. Perhaps that was inevitable. He was still expecting the police to turn up at any moment and take him in again.

He had no real idea how he had ended up in such a situation. He had no job, or wouldn't soon, so no income. He had savings but not much and the rent for his flat would swallow it up quickly. If his mother had still been alive, he could have gone back to stay with her, but that was the problem with small families like his. If one person died, there was no one left. How easy would it be to land another job in teaching after being dismissed? He'd left his job in Edinburgh under something of a cloud too after the publicity there. He didn't know who he could even ask for references now. His headmaster would hardly be feeling kindly towards him after the position Jason had put him in. No. Things were not looking good. It wasn't as if he had friends he could call on for support. He'd been on good speaking terms with one or two teachers while at school but not outside it and, for obvious reasons, he wasn't going anywhere near Isla. At least when he'd been in prison he'd known where he was or thought so anyway. He wasn't sure what situation he was in now.

But did he deserve anything else after the mess he'd made of everything? He'd killed Eddie Caldwell instead of just scaring him off, then walked out on Renée when she had needed support from him; and he'd made a fool of himself with Isla.

As he gazed at the sea, he started to find it inviting, though not from the point of view of a refreshing swim. The thought had occurred if he weighed his jacket down with stones in the pockets, and waded out, that would put an end to these emotions swirling inside him. It would be unpleasant, but the experience would come to an end, as would all his problems. Then he remembered Isla had come up with a cleverer idea than that. He had a car too and if he could direct the exhaust fumes into it with the windows closed, he would drift off to sleep and just never wake up. Though he'd have to work out how to do that. He'd have to get some sort of tube, he supposed. Isla had made it sound simple. He tried to remember what she'd said.

But perhaps he didn't deserve to reach the end of his torture so easily. He thought back to the arguments Isla had been making. Was Isla right about the healing powers of punishment? It would be good to lift the gloom that had blighted every day for so long. Would that do it – admission of guilt for something even if it wasn't his crime? If only he could ease the pain out of himself. If only he could finally relax. Perhaps he should turn himself in at the police station and confess, but he still didn't.

He'd half-hoped to run into Isla on the front but decided he was pleased he didn't. When he went back to his flat, he met Renée there. She was outside, waiting for him, which cheered him up, and he invited her in.

She lit up his dingy living-room; there was a vibrancy even in the way she arranged herself on his couch, a spark in her eyes, and when she spoke there was a decisive note in her voice.

'You couldn't have killed Tod,' she said, 'because you were with me at the time.'

'What do you mean? I was with Andy, not that he's admitting that anymore. Is that why they released me? You turned up with a false alibi?'

Jason sat down opposite her, as he tried to take her in.

'I'd almost decided to confess,' he said.

'Why on earth would you do that?'

'I'd almost convinced myself I might have done it and just not remembered it. You do read about that sort of thing. Blackouts and so on.'

'You've not lost it that much, have you?'

'Almost. They're still looking for proof against me. It's just that what they have isn't enough. It's not as if they've changed their mind about who they think did the murders.'

There was a knocking on the door, not the heavy banging there had been the last time the police called but there was an urgency to it. Jason answered nervously then discovered it was Andy. It was a weary-looking Andy, but Jason supposed they were all feeling and looking like that.

'You're here,' Andy said. 'Good. I'm glad they've released you. I saw your light on and took a chance. Can I come in?'

'Sure.'

He showed him to a seat.

'Have you met Renée?' Jason asked him. 'Andy, this is Renée. Renée, this is Andy.'

Andy shot a questioning glance in Renée's direction.

'She was my girlfriend when I was in Edinburgh.'

'Fiancée,' Renée said.

'Yes.'

Jason gave her an apologetic look.

'Pleased to meet you,' Andy said.

He looked in Jason's direction.

'Does she know about everything?'

'Yes.'

'Must be a bit of a shock,' Andy said to her.

'And then some,' Renée said.

'I was just wondering...' Andy said, and his voice faded as he pondered something. 'I've turned up here because we need to talk and sort things out. We need to work out what really happened.'

He gave Jason a questioning look.

'You've had to go through a lot I know, Jason, but it probably wasn't you – was it? They released you anyway.'

'Probably not,' Jason replied. And no thanks to you they let me go, he thought.

Andy looked at him wonderingly.

'On the other hand, you don't sound sure,' he said.

'He definitely didn't do it,' Renée said.

'She sounds convincing,' Jason said. 'I'm happy to believe her.'

Jason looked across at Renée; Andy's quizzical gaze lingered on Jason.

'Not that I've been sure of anything much for a while,' Jason said.

'Not sure about whether you killed someone or not?' Andy said and gave Jason a particularly penetrating stare.

'The police were certain for so long, I almost didn't want to disappoint them,' Jason replied.

'Oh, do,' Andy said. 'The police make mistakes. Enjoy pointing it out to them.'

'It's shocking how useless Jason can be at times,' Renée said. 'He can be a surprisingly sensitive soul.'

'I see…' Andy said, and his words tailed away again as some other thought seemed to strike him. 'Well, cheer up. If we discuss it, maybe we will find out what did happen.'

'Discuss what?' Renée said.

'We could talk about Isla for a start,' Andy said, looking at Jason. 'What's happening with her?'

'She did turn up and visit me in prison.'

'A comforting conversation, was it?'

'No. The opposite. She tried to persuade me to confess.'

'That's where that idea came from?' Renée said. 'I might have known.'

'Why would you do that?' Andy asked.

'It's complicated,' Jason said. 'But when you're having stuff thrown at you all the time, you can be worn down, you know – or maybe you don't – but the police had been at me so much about the fact that I couldn't remember anything about the night of Paul's murder, and how did I know I didn't do it? And Isla said I had an argument with Paul that night. He was warning me away from Isla. Isla says she told me Paul had hit her which is why she said I went for Paul when our tempers were up.'

'Isla's the one who's told you all this?' Andy said.

'Yes.'

'Did she say anything about Tod?'

'She said I must have planned that murder. And I'd got to the stage where I thought that if I'd forgotten about killing Paul, maybe I could have forgotten about killing Tod. I was the only one with a motive. It does sound a bit stupid now.'

'Maybe someone else did have a motive,' Andy said. 'Which is something we could chew over, along with one or two other things.'

'Which are?'

There was another knock on the door, and they looked round in surprise. Jason went to answer it and found Isla standing there. When she came in, she met hostile looks from Renée and Andy – which she ignored. Jason brought a chair through from the kitchen for her. It was crowded in Jason's tiny sitting room now and Isla's look as she glanced round suggested she didn't think much of her surroundings.

'A shareholders' meeting, is it?' she said.

'In a way,' Andy said. 'We all have a stake in what's been going on.'

'It's been difficult,' Isla said.

'What did you want to see me about?' Jason said.

But Isla had been knocked out of her stride by seeing everyone there.

'It'll wait,' she said. 'Don't let me interrupt. And who's this?'

Jason introduced her to Renée; this time he made it clear Renée had been his fiancée. Isla looked uncomfortable, but she soon recovered to give Renée a withering look which Renée returned with relish.

Andy cleared his throat to gain everyone's attention. He didn't want distractions.

'As you know,' Andy said, 'it's been in my mind before that if we could get everybody in one place and put our heads together, we could get this worked out. People have been dying. I've been trying to talk it through with Jason and Renée.'

'Sounds fine by me,' Isla said.

Andy gave Isla the opposite of a charming smile.

'Jason tells us you reckon that he did it?'

'He might have done. I don't know who killed Paul.'

'He says you said you saw him arguing with Paul.'

'I was questioning Jason.'

'That's what it was?' Jason said. 'You were making things up to get me to confess?'

When he thought about it, the idea the police might do that had come from Isla. But no. This couldn't make sense.

'Jason, you frighten me, don't you see that?' Isla said.

'Really?' was Jason's reply. 'Frighten you? I've been doing nothing but holding your hand through all your problems.'

'When you told me you'd killed that Eddie Caldwell, you scared me half to death. I was trying to get to the bottom of things,' she said.

Which was unbelievable and he wasn't surprised that Isla was starting to look uneasy. Three pairs of eyes were boring into her, Jason's with incomprehension, Renée's with anger, and Andy's with what looked like a need for retribution for something.

'I thought at first maybe you'd manipulated Jason into killing Paul for you,' Andy said, 'because you were always so good at getting people to do things for you, homework you couldn't be bothered with, telling lies to cover up for where you were when you should have been at music practice or whatever, even getting someone to have a go at someone else for you.'

'There's a difference between asking someone to help you with your homework, and persuading someone to do a murder, Andy.'

'And then some. But you'd be capable of it. We always wondered what really happened with your cousin at that weir. You said you were supposed to be meeting him there and he didn't show up. Was his problem the fact he did, then you lost your temper with him and shoved him in the water?'

'What a nasty thought,' Isla said. 'And no. That didn't happen. That whole thing really upset me. It took me years to recover from losing Leslie. How could you accuse me of that, Andy?'

But Andy was not perturbed by the reply.

'We'll never know what that row was about,' Andy said. 'Leslie can't tell us now.'

'If he could, he'd tell you there wasn't one.'

'It probably was an accident,' Jason said, 'if that's what everybody decided at the time. It's not fair accusing Isla of that now.'

'Maybe you should listen to Andy,' Renée said. 'You don't see through Isla even now, do you, Jason?'

Isla looked daggers at Renée.

'Just because you couldn't hold onto Jason,' she said, 'don't take it out on me.'

'We'll never be able to prove anything about Leslie's death,' Andy said. 'They couldn't at the time. But we can talk about Tod's death, and that would be a good one to start with because if Jason didn't kill Tod – and it doesn't look as if he did – whoever killed Tod was attempting to implicate Jason. And you were trying to persuade Jason to confess.'

'You mean I did it?' Isla said. 'That's another leap in the dark. How long have you known me? Jason did it. He's the one with the reason to. That's why I was trying to get him to confess. To give the rest of us a break.'

Andy didn't look convinced.

'If you killed Tod, Isla, it means you killed Paul, because Tod's murder was one intended to be pinned on Jason to make him look guilty of Paul's. I've known you a long time, Isla. You're capable of being Paul's murderer. You're great company, none better, but suddenly you just change, don't you? You don't get your own way, or you take offence, and you snap. We've seen it often enough – Isla, she of the dulcet tones and the sweet smile turning into Isla the furious fishwife. And you're capable of anything when you snap. You could easily have killed Paul, and then needed to cover it up.'

Which Jason considered for the first time might be true. He had seen her snapping in an argument with Joanne.

'Really?' Isla said.

'Yes. And death has always followed you around, hasn't it, Isla? First, your mother, whom I don't suggest that you killed, but her death did affect you. It taught you how close we all are to death. But I don't think Leslie died in an accident. He was your first murder. Which was when you learned something else. You could get away with it.'

'You've a good imagination, Andy,' Isla said. 'You should take up writing stories.'

'You argued with Leslie – about something, anything, maybe nothing. But you snapped. Maybe you hadn't planned it beforehand, but you did intend to kill him when you pushed him into that weir. You pretended to have a nervous breakdown afterwards so that no one would think you could have done it. And having killed before, you found it much easier to do it again, didn't you? You and Paul were both unfaithful to each other. But especially Paul. And it must have irked.'

'I see it,' Renée said. 'I'm getting to know you. Maybe you snapped when you killed Leslie, but you didn't need to snap to kill after that. You planned the rest, didn't you?'

'Definitely,' Andy said. 'I always wondered what she saw in Jason. Not that there's anything wrong with him. He's a decent guy. But he's not posh. Isla's friends are all posh. But you noticed Jason around, didn't you, Isla? And then somehow you found out about Eddie Caldwell and thought how useful Jason could be to you, so you invited him around to your pool party, the one where you planned to murder Paul once you'd got the band to play in the music room and everyone was busy dancing. And you spiked Jason's drink so he wouldn't be able to remember anything.'

Then things started coming back to Jason. It was strange that should happen now. Or possibly not, with all this discussion and all these heated emotions. There had been an argument with Paul. Jason remembered it clearly now and he hadn't been the one arguing with him. Nor had it been Lena or Amber. It had been Isla. She'd been going on at him about Joanne. Nobody was even noticing Jason; nobody'd known him after all. He'd just met Isla so it didn't make sense that Paul would be angry with him about Isla. Jason hadn't seen Isla delivering the blow, but she must have been the one to do it. The drink – with whatever had been added to it – must have taken its toll on him about then. Perhaps Isla had intended it to take effect before. She couldn't have meant him to witness the argument with Paul. Or maybe that had erupted before schedule.

Andy continued.

'You'd always planned that Jason should take the blame for Paul's murder. He'd killed someone before in an argument about a girl. So why couldn't he have done it in an argument with Paul over you? So, you befriended Jason in as public a way as you could think, so that everyone would think you must always have been lovers, and suspect Jason because he did after all look as if he had a motive.'

Isla looked across at Jason.

'I'm not that kind of person. Really. I didn't do any of that.'

'Oh, but you are, Isla,' Andy said.

There was a great certainty in the way Andy was talking and Jason was believing every word.

'I've known you in a lot of situations. You fall for guys. You fall out with guys. You use guys. You soar to the heights of happiness. You dive to the depths of despair. You go through every emotion imaginable, come across as the exact opposite of what everyone would think of as a psychopath, except there's one emotion I've never ever seen in you. Genuine empathy. Oh, you can feign it – when you remember – but not well. It's not something you've ever experienced. You could kill someone and never even notice it. You felt bad after Leslie's death, but not because you were feeling for Leslie, only for yourself – because you were worrying about being caught.'

'As if the great Andy would know anything about empathy. You're a lawyer. They're cold fish. They are. Every single one.'

'And there was that girl at your school that died, wasn't there, Isla? Wherever you go, you scatter death around like breadcrumbs. She was supposed to have been killed by that male rapist and murderer active in that area, that Lomax fellow, the only problem being that was the one murder he never admitted to. What were you falling out with her about, Isla, when you snapped?'

Now Jason found himself looking at Isla with horror.

'This is fantasy, Andy – and you'll never prove any of it,' Isla said.

'Is it? I've always wondered about the death of that girl. That's why I was so determined to find out what was going on here. As you know so well, she was my sister.'

Then there was silence and the atmosphere between Andy and Isla was deadly. Jason and Renée were still trying to take in the last revelation.

'I'm sorry about your sister,' Isla said. 'But it wasn't me. Truly it wasn't.'

But there was guilt written all over Isla's face, as far as Jason could see; even as she flashed her charming smile.

'Which is why you'll never ever prove that it was me. And you'll never be able to prove anything else either.'

A hysterical laugh came out of Andy – and it was strange coming from him.

'You're right,' he said, 'and, if I had it in me, I should kill you. It's the only way to bring all this to an end.'

Then Isla stood up and strode to the door. She turned and flashed them all a smile. And it was one of her more enchanting smiles. Suddenly she was the Isla that Jason had first met, she of the violet eyes and the bewilderingly white teeth. All her confidence and pertness had returned, and she was mocking them. Then she turned again and left.

Jason turned to Andy.

'You're right,' Jason said. 'You've got it all worked out. Clever man. And what a horror she is. Why didn't I see it? But there isn't any proof against her, is there?'

'No. There isn't,' Andy said.

'But you're not going to kill her, are you?' Renée said.

Andy did not reply and Renée gave Jason an anxious stare, one that echoed his own uncertainties. Andy didn't stay long after that. With a self-absorbed look on his face, he excused himself and departed.

'I hope they nail her,' Renée said. 'She's dangerous.'

'I hadn't seen it,' Jason said.

'You wouldn't,' Renée told him. 'And she's the real deal. The definition of psycho. Maybe you never do see them coming. And she would have made sure you took the blame for her murders. If she gets the chance, she still will.'

'After that?' Jason said.

'After what? She didn't confess. You're right. Andy's got it worked out, but it's as she said, he has no evidence.'

'So where does that leave me?'

'Hoping the police can't assemble a better case against you. And if she can give them anything to help them, she will.'

'If Andy goes to them about Isla, they'll have to investigate her.'

'He should. He was strange though, don't you think? Just walked out without talking about any of what just happened there. Where do you think he's gone? Do you think he has gone to the police station?'

'I don't know.'

'Should we have gone after him?' Renée said.

'I don't know.'

Jason looked back at her. That was all they did for a few moments, look vacantly at each other, and they didn't go after Andy.

'What do you plan to do next?' Renée asked him.

'I don't know. It's finished for me here.'

'Why don't you come back down to Edinburgh?'

It sounded such a good idea. Jason looked at Renée as he contemplated her.

'I've treated you dreadfully,' he said. 'I came up here to try to escape and I didn't need to because I had you.'

He'd been so stupid. He'd doubted her when the one who'd been manipulating him all along had been Isla. Then he and Renée were in each other's arms, and he realised Renée had been the one who'd reached out to him. What a relief, and how great to have hope back in his life again. They could only try with each other. He certainly would.

* * *

Of course, he couldn't up sticks and leave just like that. There were various things to be organized. The rented flat was furnished so there were no problems about what to do with furniture and so on, but it was surprising how much stuff he had; he was going to have a full carload. He settled up with his landlord and made arrangements about the electricity and gas bills to come, let his school know he was leaving the area and would give them an address later, and that was that. He would not bother attending his 'hearing'. The school could just dismiss him if it wished, which it would. It had taken a surprising amount of time to think all that through, and the whole ordeal surrounding the murders had left him feeling off-balance, so it was great to think he and Renée were back together.

It felt so positive to be organizing his next step. It occurred to him that he ought to let the police know what he was doing as they'd declared him a person of such interest in their inquiries. When he phoned them, the response was not what he wanted.

'It's odd you're thinking of leaving at this precise moment,' he was told after he had eventually got through to someone involved in The Poolside Murder inquiry – and it was Buchanan himself.

'Why do you say that?' Jason asked.

'We were about to ask you more questions.'

That answer filled him with dread. Had Isla been giving them more leads? He had so wanted to escape from all of this. Would he ever?

'I've told you everything,' he said. 'Well, no. I've recovered my memories of that night. I haven't told you about that yet, but I can now. It was Isla who was having the argument with Paul, which was about Joanne. Paul had been having an affair with her and Isla objected. I got fed up of listening and wandered off to another room, found a couch, and succumbed to whatever was in my Manhattan. End of story.'

It had been a relief when the rest of his memories had returned as he hadn't known if they ever would – and he was glad that they didn't include him murdering Paul.

'You didn't see the murder?'

'No. Sorry. But it must have been Isla as she was the one having the row with Paul.'

'That's interesting, sir.'

Jason supposed it was fascinating, but he didn't see the point in Buchanan saying that.

'Because Isla has been found dead now.'

Jason was stunned.

'Isla,' he said. 'I don't believe you.'

'She was hit by a car,' Buchanan said. 'A hit and run. So don't leave town yet because we'll want to talk to you again soon – when we've finished establishing the facts about the accident.'

'I see.'

And Jason's heart fell. He supposed he had a motive for that one: Isla had been trying to frame him. Though he wasn't sure if the police were aware of that. It was becoming complicated, too complicated for him. When Buchanan had finished, he put the phone down and turned to Renée.

'What was all that about?' she asked.

'Nothing good,' he said. 'Isla's been found dead – in a hit and run. The police are still investigating.'

'Someone killed her on purpose?'

'It would be too much of a coincidence otherwise,' Jason said.

'What was it Andy said?' Renée asked.

Jason thought.

'What were his exact words?'

'I don't remember,' Jason replied. 'But he did say killing Isla would be the only way to bring this to an end.'

'So, Andy killed her,' Renée said. 'And I liked him.'

'I thought it was talk,' Jason said. 'Andy was all right. But it must have been an awful shock to think it was Isla who'd done that to his sister.'

'As well as her other killings. We've got to do what we can to help him.'

'Like what?'

'We don't tell the police about Andy's threat to kill Isla.'

'I've had a lot to do with the police lately and they were difficult enough to deal with when I was telling the truth. I dread to think what they'd be like if I started lying to them. Presumably we can tell them the rest of the conversation?'

'Yes.'

'In any case—' he didn't finish the sentence straight away '—you do realise who the other suspect for Isla's death is? Isla was trying to set me up to take the blame for her murders, which gives me all the motive in the world to kill her.'

As Renée looked back at him, he could see that the logic had not been wasted on her, though her mind was obviously still working on it.

'Do you think the police have got that figured out?' she said.

Then something else struck her.

'We thought Isla was the murderer,' she said. 'We thought she'd killed Paul and Tod, but could this mean we were wrong? Could the same person have killed her as well?'

'And it wasn't Andy who murdered Isla?'

'Yes.'

'Neither of us thought he would do it. He said he didn't think he could, didn't he?'

'We didn't believe her when she said she was innocent, but Isla didn't admit to anything. Could it have been someone else doing the murders?'

They shared a silence as even Jason had a moment of doubt. Then his thought went back to his oh-so-real memories of that argument.

'Who else would it have been?' Jason said.

TWENTY-FIVE

Jason was back on the seafront, which seemed to draw him like a magnet every time he needed space to think. He was on his own. Renée had objected to him going off like this as well she might. He'd had rather too much personal space over the last few months. But anyway, here he was, on a bench he had once shared with Isla, looking over the sea and pondering her. Then Mark turned up and sat beside him.

'I'm sorry about your loss,' Jason said.

'I'm sorry about yours,' Mark said. 'She must have come to mean a lot to you.'

'Yes.'

Mark couldn't have realised the conclusions the rest of them had been coming to and Jason didn't like to tell him. An uncomfortable silence settled. As they sat looking out to sea. Jason tried to make his thoughts go elsewhere but there was no escaping the dreadfulness of the situation. They must have made a sad-looking pair, with no sign of a smile anywhere, even on Mark's face.

Jason was pondering him. Mark did look upset after Isla's death but Jason found himself wondering how real it was. Mark was an actor. There had been obvious tension between him and Paul. But Tod's murder made no sense – unless it had been Mark trying to set Jason up as the murderer. Jason didn't want to think that. He'd liked Mark. In any case, there had been the quarrel between Isla and Paul. That was conclusive, wasn't it?

'You do know Isla was trying to frame you, don't you?' Mark said.

That was straight to the point and Jason looked at him with surprise.

'It was suggested to me,' Jason said.

'I won't ask by whom,' Mark said. 'I don't want to interrogate you. You've been through enough.'

Indeed he had, Jason thought, though he doubted if Mark could appreciate how much.

'There have been so many deaths,' Mark said.

'Yes.'

'They seemed to happen wherever Isla went.'

Mark paused as he allowed the implications of this to sink in. When he started speaking again, the voice was gentle, as if he was explaining something to a child.

'She was always a strange girl,' he said. 'She had a very unusual way of playing with dolls. She fussed over them so. Quite often she wasn't satisfied with the clothes the manufacturer had put on them and found others that she thought suited the doll better. And she would improve the make-up, even cut the hair slightly differently. And when she thought she'd made her doll perfect, she would start doing her role plays with it. She had a voice for every doll and a personality. And she made them do things for her, like help her with her homework. All pretend, of course. Then when the teacher wasn't satisfied with the homework, she would punish the doll. She was so caring with her dolls and so bossy – and so brutal. She really made them suffer – if dolls can be said to do that.

'She had quite a temper when she was young. When she didn't get her own way, she had dreadful tantrums. And she never grew out of them.

'We were puzzled when we first found one of her dolls mutilated. We thought some friend of Isla's must have done it, but no. It was Isla. When she was in trouble about something, she would storm off and take her temper out on her doll. Isla had a flash point that she reached. She could be so nicey-nice, such good company, but then she would change for whatever reason. You usually couldn't see it coming. She would be annoyed sometimes about one thing and then about another. And it was as if she became a different person. There was so much fury in her and she didn't know how to get rid of it. We thought taking it out on her dolls was at least harmless enough, silly even. But, you know... you were one of her dolls.'

'What?' Jason said.

'You were a plaything to her. I know it's an odd thing to say but she was a bit like that with Leslie as well. She would get him to do things for her, but when what he did wasn't good enough, wow, the temper. It didn't occur to me at first you were another Leslie to her, but when it did, it worried me. I never believed in my heart of hearts that Leslie's death was an accident. I didn't want to believe Isla had killed him, but it was always a suspicion in my mind.

'She must have become interested in you when she realised you had killed someone. And as I said, you look like Leslie. She talked about you before she invited you to that pool party. That wasn't out of the blue.

'It was after Paul's murder that I realised what she must have been up to with you. It occurred to me Isla must have killed Paul. Who benefits? Isn't that the question the police always ask? And Isla did. Not that I wanted to believe it. No. Isla couldn't have done that. So, I dismissed the thought for long enough. But Paul was a waste of space. I'd told her that before she married him. The problem was she was so self-willed. And he played around with other women dreadfully, which Isla pretended didn't bother her, but Isla wasn't like that. If Paul was hers, she wouldn't share him with anyone. Maybe, just maybe, she could forgive him for one affair but not all of those, and not with her best friend Joanne. And once someone had crossed Isla they were in trouble. She had her revenge. In the end, I just had to believe it.

'Jason, she cultivated you and manipulated you so you would become the main suspect. After all, you'd killed before.

'Then Tod was killed, of course. And just to implicate you? What was wrong with Tod? It wasn't even as if he'd ever done anything to Isla. As if that would have justified it anyway.

'She was my daughter and when I couldn't blind myself anymore to what she was doing, and the kind of person she had grown into, I was devastated. I couldn't let it go on. She was killing people, and once she'd learned to do that, she was never going to stop.

'I've always tried so hard to look out for her. It was terrible when her mother died right beside her in that car crash. Maybe that was what did it to her, I don't know. Or maybe it was just what she was like.'

It was then that Jason realised what Mark was doing: he was confessing to Isla's murder.

'Isla's accident wasn't that difficult to arrange. I've been in enough action movies. Movie directors don't realise the skills they're teaching actors, not that I ever expected to make use of them. It was just the best thing I could think of to do for her. I couldn't bear the thought of a court trial and Isla going to prison. And isn't it dreadful? That was the best thing I could do for my daughter.'

A tear started coursing down Mark's cheek.

'It won't come back to hurt you. Don't worry about it. It won't come back to me either.'

Jason had to feel for him. Mark Landy. Jason had thought at one point he'd never really seen him for the perfect impression he insisted on giving to the world. But Jason could see beyond the smile now. And he realised where Isla got her ruthlessness from, as well as her good looks. Not that he supposed Mark had killed before. But he'd found himself eminently capable of it. Then another thought occurred to Jason. Just how much had Isla taken after her father? If she'd been convicted of the murders, there would have been so much bad publicity Mark's career would have been finished. Was that why Mark had killed Isla? Surely not. No. What Mark had said did make sense. Didn't it?

'Has Andy talked to you?' Jason asked.

'Andy? What about?'

'He worked out what Isla had been doing too. And there's something more.'

'More?'

'Something about his sister. She was killed – by a serial rapist and murderer supposedly who confessed to other crimes in the area, but not that one. And if Isla's been doing all these other murders, that must have been her as well. At least that's what Andy decided. Which is why we thought maybe it was Andy who killed Isla. We hadn't thought it might be you.'

'We?'

'Me and Reneé. She was my fiancée in Edinburgh. She's looked me up again.'

'I'm glad you've got her. I hope it works out for you. But Andy's sister, did he really think Isla did that one?'

Mark pondered for a while.

'Yes. She could have done. I hadn't thought about that. It seemed so cut and dry. That one was added to all those other crimes that man did because it fitted in.'

Then he pondered again.

'No. The police won't come after Andy. They won't connect him to this.'

Then another silence fell, and then Mark started talking about Isla again.

'I'll miss her so much,' he said, and Jason found himself believing him. 'I daresay you will too. She was a fetching girl with such life in her and I don't know how I'll live with myself after what I've done now. But it had to be done, didn't it?'

He gave Jason a look that was appealing for something, anything from Jason, understanding, or forgiveness. And it was heart-wrenching.

'Yes,' Jason said. 'I'll miss Isla.'

He thought of her smile again, and her eyes.

'But the things she was doing,' Jason said. 'She couldn't go on doing that.'

Jason's words looked as if they helped Mark – to some extent – though there was still so much pain in his face. It was a pain that Jason knew something about, one that would not leave easily, the pain of taking someone else's life. Killing Isla had cost Mark. Definitely.

Mark had reached the end of all he'd come to say, and there were no magical words of comfort Jason could think of. Both he and Mark sat looking out over the water for a while before muttering polite and meaningless things and leaving each other with embarrassed and sorrowful looks on their faces.

Jason did feel for Mark. He'd thought him the man with everything, so much money, so much fame, and such a beautiful daughter.

TWENTY-SIX

It was an uncomfortable thought to Jason – how he must have appeared to Isla as he'd looked enviously at her and her gilded set of friends on Nairn shorefront. He'd been a lamb to the slaughter. At least everything was over now. The police had decided the car accident was just that. Isla had been upset by everything she'd been going through and had been wandering around much in her own thoughts when she'd walked in front of a speeding car. It was considered an unhappy accident but that was all. Of course, the driver had committed a crime by not stopping but neither he nor the car were ever traced. There was no need to bother Jason with further questions so he was free to go.

Jason wondered if the police were laying the blame for Paul and Tod's murders at her door now, which was where it belonged, but he wasn't told anything about their thoughts on those, and he did not care about that much. All that mattered to Jason was that they seemed to have stopped trying to blame him.

When he'd loaded his car and locked the door to his flat for the last time, he decided he wanted to have one last look at Nairn seafront so that he could say goodbye to it. After all, so many meaningful moments had happened beside it. Renée acquiesced happily enough. They drove down and parked there to look out at the sea.

It was a fine day, the sea was calm, the sky blue, and the sun was shining. Looking out over the firth was a treat.

'I can see why you liked it here,' Renée said.

'It should have been good,' Jason said. 'But it would never have been enough.'

'Wouldn't it?'

'Not without you.'

That was a good thought. There was peace between him and Renée. They were together, and he knew she had none of the hidden depths of Isla. Renée was uncomplicated and just what she seemed. And he really hoped she was going to stay that way.

'Good. I'm glad you think that,' Renée said.

'And I can stop running away now,' Jason said.

'That's not what you're doing now?' Renée asked.

'Not at all,' Jason said. 'I'm running towards something. I'm running towards you.'

'I'm glad you feel like that.'

Jason paused as he thought some more.

'I feel at peace with myself for the first time in a long time,' he said, 'so there might be something of me for someone else now.'

'There always was. You just didn't know it.'

'Well, there's more anyway. I've finally forgiven myself.'

'For what?'

'For Eddie's death. It was an accident.'

'That's what everyone told you. You were the only one who didn't realise it.'

'I branded myself a murderer in my own mind with that. But I'm not. I know now what a murderer looks like. They have violet eyes,' he said, 'and a wonderful smile. And they carry death about with them like an afterthought. It means nothing to them at all. And I'm nothing like that.'

AUTHOR'S NOTE

Nairn is a town that does exist; it is on the north coast of Scotland, sixteen miles east of Inverness. Though Nairn itself is real, certain elements of the Nairn in the novel are fictional.

This is a contemporary novel and the murder in *Where Wolves Prowl* takes place in a striking modernist eco-house on Nairn seafront. Along the shore at Nairn are some rather grand houses, including a couple of modernistic ones so that, though the one in the novel does not exist, it is easy to imagine one like it in that setting.

The fictional house belongs to a fictional film actor, Mark Landy. It might seem to be stretching the imagination to its limits to place the house of a film actor in a Scottish seaside town, but there is one at present living in Nairn, Tilda Swinton, even if she is the complete opposite of Mark Landy, my Scottish action movie star. There may be no Mark Landy as such living in Nairn, but one might be possible. After all, Charlie Chaplin is known to have spent his holidays in Nairn, and Margaret Rutherford and Burt Lancaster are purported to have visited.

Likewise, the private school outside Nairn that Jason Sutherland teaches in does not exist. There was one in Nairn called Alton Burn School, which thrived from the 1890s to the 1930s, and there is one in Forres now, ten miles from Nairn, so the one in the novel could be possible. There is, of course, a local authority high school but I did not want to have Jason Sutherland teaching there as there are real teachers in that school and real pupils and I did not want any of them wondering if anyone they know is in the novel. All of the characters and events in the novel are fictitious.

If you enjoyed this book, please let others know by leaving a quick review on Amazon. Also, if you spot anything untoward in the paperback, get in touch. We strive for the best quality and appreciate reader feedback.

editor@thebookfolks.com

www.thebookfolks.com

MORE FICTION BY JAMES ANDREW

The Yorkshire Murders series:

The Body Under The Sands
Death Waits For No Lady
The Riddle Of The Dunes
The Suitcase Murderer

Standalone mysteries:

Burning Suspicion

All of these books are available free with Kindle Unlimited and in paperback.

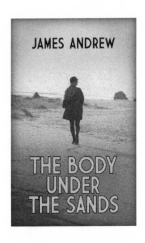

The Body Under The Sands

Book 1 of The Yorkshire Murders series

Two soldiers recently returned from the Great War are accused of murdering a woman near a small seaside town. They protest their innocence but are convicted on circumstantial evidence and given the death penalty. One of the soldiers begins to suspect the other as guilty. But can he betray his brother in arms who saved his life during the war?

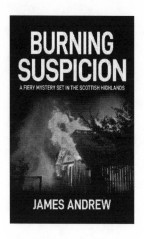

Burning Suspicion

A standalone mystery

Following James Andrew's powerful historical mystery
series set in Yorkshire, this is a mystery set closer to home
in the Highlands.
When their house is burned down, a family starts to turn
on one another – but who was the arsonist and what was
burning them up? A truly gripping read.

OTHER TITLES OF INTEREST

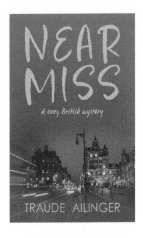

Near Miss

The debut mystery by Traude Ailinger

After being nearly hit by a car, fashion journalist Amy Thornton decides to visit the driver, who ends up in hospital after evading her. Curious about this strange man she becomes convinced she's unveiled a murder plot. But it won't be so easy to persuade Scottish detective DI Russell McCord.

Free with Kindle Unlimited and available in paperback from Amazon.

Don't Go Back

Debut psychological fiction by Mark West

Beth's partner Nick can't quite understand why she acts so strangely when they return to her hometown for the funeral of a once-close friend. But she hasn't told him everything about her past. Memories of one terrible summer will come flooding back to her. And with them, violence and revenge.

FREE with Kindle Unlimited and available in paperback from Amazon.

Made in the USA
Middletown, DE
24 June 2022

67645517R00111